THE LAST WAR
WE EVER FOUGHT

a love story

WENDY HEISS

BLUE FAIRYTALE NOVELS

Heiss Publishing

Book cover Illustrator: Katerina Zaitseva

Book cover designer: Margherita Scialla

www.wendyheissauthor.com

Author Blurbs

"This story contains all elements one would love in a retelling of a classical fairy tale or beloved myth, and yet is as original as it is raw and vulnerable. Rowan and Elijah share a love story that follows them throughout lifetimes and will haunt the readers long after closing this book."

-Lauren Dedroog, Author of A Curse Of Crows

"Heiss's The Last War We Ever Fought marks a fairytale renaissance in fantasy, presenting a lush novella that beautifully captures the dark side of victory, love, and loss, igniting a desire for more."

-J.D. Ronan, Author of A Deadly Vow

For whoever will still like me after reading this book.

Foreword

The novellas in this series are considered love stories, they are not categorised as romance or *romantasy* or fantasy romance even though there are elements of both fantasy and romance (the closest category it can be placed is *literary romance* with elements of fantasy). I feel that I have to specify that they are not plot heavy, nor is the plot a main focus. These are just a few short stories focusing on two people in love, with characterization as a main focus. The intention for the story was to be fast paced, sweet, and short.

Content warnings

War, genocide, murder, depression, scars, death, blood.
   Explicit content (18+)

Contents

One poppy

MANKIND HAD FOUGHT. SINCE birth, it was all it had done. Fought to breathe. Fought to survive. Fought to feed. Fought to learn. It was between those lines that Elijah had turned from merely a servant of man to a God. Fights had turned into conflicts. Conflicts had turned into war. And a ghostly presence had turned into the most ruthless deity to exist.

He'd lived many lifetimes no man would ever outlive. But he'd finally lived one where soon, there would be no more war to live through.

Man had almost won over man in the small realm of Tisiania. A realm made of only one large stretch of earth and inhabited by two nations that had been each other's peril since the beginning of its existence. The Gobresh and the Mugril. The north and the south.

Humankind was about to fight its very last war on Tisiania.

All because of her.

Because of what he was seeing.

Because of what he'd never seen before.

He stood at the feet of the last battle, rain pattering against this dark armour, hissing and twisting into mist at the contact. The soil was freshly bloodied. The bodies were not yet cold. It was empty of most human life, and the invisible hounds of *Death* were already prowling over the spirits and leading them towards the path of the afterlife. Most human life belonging to the Mugril side had gone to celebrate their win. Jolly voices, clicks of metal cups filled to the brim with liquor, and odes to battle being sung. Most life sought life. Gathered around it to celebrate another day they'd been spared. Gone to celebrate their crimes against their own kind. Gone to celebrate their desire to see the Gobresh extinct.

Most. Not all.

One life remained. A half-life rather.

Elijah couldn't figure out why the human was moving when he felt so little life from her. Perhaps she'd been injured. But then, it couldn't be that.

The woman had shed most of her armour and weapons, her dark brown braided hair no longer contained to the bind, curls soaking in the thin drizzle that had just begun to taint the already cold evening. Elijah couldn't tell her features behind all the blood and grime that had clung to her face. The only thing he could see were her eyes. A vivid green. The coldest green he'd ever seen. Inanimate. Distant. Almost resembling a corpse.

She dug her dozenth too shallow of a hole and pulled another body into it before lowering at the edge and murmuring what Elijah could only guess was a prayer.

He had watched her for the past couple hours repeat the same thing over and over. Burying bodies he'd seen her soldiers kill, burying bodies she herself had ordered to be killed. None belonging to her side of the war.

Elijah had remained there, still unsure of what he was seeing. Or who.

By the time the skies were losing their pity on the human pane and their desire to see, the woman had cleared almost half of the battlefield. She dragged her tired limbs to the last grave, her knees dropping with a thud in the mud, too exhausted to obey her orders.

Her cold eyes drew shut and her body gave up entirely, letting her collapse on top of the corpses piling inside the last shallow grave she'd made.

"Rowan," someone called through the chilling night air. The boy was young, but just old enough to belong in a battlefield. He rushed to her, pulling her limp, half lifeless body out of the grave and then retching his stomach open from the stench of rotting and blood that had clung to her.

She laid on the mud, her bloodied and chaffed fingers twitching against the soft surface. Barely able to peel and pull herself up, Rowan patted a hand to the boy's back, soothing him. "Why aren't you resting already?" she asked, her voice hoarse and sunken to a depth Elijah couldn't figure how deep it was just yet.

The boy heaved, tears clinging to his eyes when he realised she was not dead. "The other generals were looking for you," he said, almost sobbing.

"Thought they'd be drunk enough by now and forgotten about me."

"They drank in your honour all afternoon. We won because of you, and you weren't even there."

Her head lowered, her shoulders shaking as she laughed or cried. There were tears in her eyes, but she was wearing the wildest grin Elijah had ever seen. She laughed. And laughed. Cried, too. Once she was sated, she planted a palm on the muddy floor and pushed herself up to stand, struggling and testing her legs before fully trusting them to hold her body up.

"We won?" she asked him, pushing his helping hand away from her as if it had burned her. "Where? Show me where."

The boy tried to hide his frown and held back his words by pressing his mouth shut.

The two looked like old friends. From the way they spoke and understood each other with only simple stares and easy gestures, perhaps they were even more than friends.

"You should join them, Rowan," he said, just as she made her way towards the tents their party had erected by the battlefield. "The war will soon be over, and they will have no need for us unless we make them think they do."

"If I cared to be useful to this war, Daniel, I would have killed myself a long time ago."

"You're their weapon. Like it or not. *You* won this battle, and *you* will help them win this war."

She laughed again, a little more cruelly this time. Not even deigning a response to who had almost appeared to be someone she was close to.

Elijah didn't know why he followed after her towards the camp. And it had seemed like the longest walk he'd ever been on. Rowan had stumbled, ached, and bled all the way to her tent set on the far corner of the camp, somewhat distanced from the rest.

He'd stood there, outside of her space, unmoving. Hearing her quick breaths and muffled whimpers as she'd cleaned herself up and bandaged all of her wounds.

Her small sounds of pain and grief clashing against the sounds of victory and joy. Such a stark contrast even to his ancient senses.

The cheers from close by and the out of tune sound of string instruments seemed a faraway world from the one inside the tent.

Steps coming from behind him made Elijah turn.

The boy from before, Daniel, startled at his sight, wide eyed and scrambling away from him while blindly reaching for weapons he did not have on him. He stopped once he got a glimpse at the sword Elijah was carrying on his back. There was awe and horror on his face as he studied the blade. "It cannot be."

The steel Elijah carried was not like most. The blade was a strange shade of silver that reflected many colours when light hit it, and the hilt was engraved with poppies and ruby diamonds made of blood spilled from godly veins—his own godly veins. He liked to remind himself sometimes that he could still bleed.

He carried the sword that was forged at the dawn of time by fates to be gifted to the King of Gods. Gifted to him. *Dawnbringer* was its name.

"Humans always have such ways of coping with what they fear. Wishing it away isn't the greatest one," Elijah said, his gaze returning to the woman who'd just come out of her tent and headed to join the celebrations despite what he'd seen and heard merely minutes ago.

The boy, Daniel, still seemed to struggle to comprehend his presence. "It would mean—"

Elijah watched Rowan avoid all praise and greetings, taking a seat by one of the generals around the massive campfire. "It means the end."

"B-but it can't be the end."

"This one won't go away, Daniel. Don't waste your wishing."

A slow smile pulled over his face, one full of cruel realisation. "Will this mean we win the war?"

"I'm not fate. Only a God."

Wide eyed and exhilarated, Daniel backed away towards the celebrations, watching Elijah over his shoulders from time to time as if to make sure he'd not hallucinated the interaction.

Elijah watched the boy animatedly shout and gesture towards him until the celebrations went quiet and every attention turned in his direction.

He could feel a pair of soulless eyes looking at him amongst the many lively ones. Her gaze was like a heavy burden somehow. Like a wound festering. Something he should feel guilty about but could never know why. The more she looked at him, the more he noticed something that entranced him entirely. A spark. Heatless. Cold. Dead. But it was a spark, nonetheless. Something made entirely out of...hate.

At that realisation, Elijah couldn't help but smile. No one

hated war. Not really. They feared it. They wished it away. But they didn't hate it. Because deep down, humanity knew of its own faults, of its own desires that had made Elijah one of the most powerful Gods.

She hated him.

And it was entirely too fascinating to him.

The look of hate turned into contemplation, and agitation was obvious in the way her fingers drummed against her thigh and how her chest rose fast enough to call upon a storm.

Elijah was curious about what she would do. Would she act on her hate like she was wanting to?

Just when she was about to take a step towards him, an older soldier stepped before her, blocking her from his sight.

"She is one of our generals," Daniel said, noticing his gaze as he ran to him with a cup of something that resembled piss. "Adam and Henry deal with training, she is the strategist."

"The strategist?" War asked, throwing the drink to the ground.

He nodded, frowning at the spilled drink that also smelled like piss to Elijah. "She levels the playing fields. Plans sabotage. She studies the enemy's weakness, from their food they eat to the clothes they wear. Once she made us block a town's path all night long with rocks we rolled from the hills because she figured out the land under the battlefield we'd meet their army was loess sediment and it had been raining hard for a couple weeks. They were then forced to evade the blocked road by taking the straight path up the hill. Half of their soldiers were stuck in the mud while the other half had already given up the climb, too tired to even fight. We took that town in less than a day, raising less swords than during crowning celebrations."

Elijah had stunned.

The human was cheating him.

She was cheating war.

The human had figured a way into cheating the God of War and no one knew—no one knew she had found a way to weaken him.

"The little thief," he murmured to himself, watching the older soldier lead her inside a tent.

She spared him one last scathing glance over her shoulder and ducked out of sight.

That made him chuckle. It had been a long while since he'd felt so entertained.

"Rowan," he spoke her name to the autumn wind, and then waited to watch if it would shiver.

It did.

Two poppies

ROWAN'S MIND WAS FAR away from where everyone else's inside the main tent was. She was still refusing to believe her ears and the words Daniel had screamed on top of his lungs for all the camp to hear.

The God of War was here himself. Dawnbringer strapped to the back of his black armour that looked more etched to his body than worn.

He'd looked at her, too. He'd looked at her as if she was something that belonged to him. And maybe she did.

He was *war*, and Rowan was his blade. She'd been his blade since the age of six, freshly orphaned after both her parents had died fighting the same war she was now fighting. Shortly after she'd buried her mother and father, she'd been made to join the war, too. Kitchens and then the infirmary, bandaging severed limbs and praying when they'd run out of medication. And soon after, at barely eleven years old, she'd been thrown in the training grounds, made to hold a weapon twice her weight and endure pain twice what her brittle bones could withhold without being too far gone for repair. Fifteen years later, she had lost count of how many times she'd been made to withstand that pain. She'd also lost sense of the weight of her weapon as she'd grown into her body. A body that had been kind to her despite how unkind she'd been to it. She'd grown past what most female soldiers grew to be, and at five feet and ten inches tall, she could disguise herself fairly well between the men. Well enough that the generals had promoted her into rank after rank without taking notice, and had now somehow sat her on an important decision-making seat that wrote the fate of the thirty-two regiments they were leading down to Gobresh. Rowan had very little sense of vanity, she couldn't remember the last time she'd faced a mirror, or even remember how she looked, not that there was much to look at beneath the grime and the grimness, but she'd been a little offended when the other general, Adam, had only found out she was a woman several months after she'd been in the position.

And as Adam spoke of their next move towards the southern land they were to take next, Rowan couldn't look away from the reflection of her eyes on the blade she held before her. She'd seen death. She'd seen so much death. All kinds of it. But she was struggling to understand what kind of death her eyes had died to look so far gone from the world of the living. There was nothing in them. Not even a faint memory or ghost of them.

She twisted and twisted the blade, as if some other angle of the reflection would find the life that she was not sure if it had even been there in the first place. A silent gasp was trapped between her slightly parted lips when another figure joined the reflection on the blade. Frozen, Rowan could only stare at the figure of the man with long dark hair and such violent violet eyes that sent a tremble down her spine. His gaze had pinned Rowan's, trapped it in the blade she held because she was unable to look elsewhere. Surely, he'd conjured some curse, a deadly glamour that wouldn't allow her to look away until she'd wither and die, because Rowan could almost feel the crawl of death pulling onto her fingertips. But the call of death was mercy. A call of desperation, a call as if to come to her rescue. Rescue from him. He was far worse than death—at least *Death* was a gentler God.

A warm trickle of liquid touched the finger that held the tip of the blade. It trailed down her hand and past her sleeve, soaking her wool shirt that was already far too warm against her skin.

"You're bleeding," a haunting dark voice called, and the ringing in her ears seized, the spell of her frozen body fled, and her lungs moved fast to steal the air around as if it was finite.

Rowan's eyes darted away from the reflection on the blade to the small wound on her fingertip that gushed with blood. Quickly, she wiped the cut on her trousers, and spun around to look at the man. But there was no man before her. He was no man. Even without his terrifying obsidian armour or sword, he would never look like a man.

"Rowan," he said her name as if he was walking through fire.

She looked around the now empty tent, wondering how long she'd been looking at that reflection in the blade to not have noticed the time that had passed or that she was now alone with him. "Yes?"

"You're still bleeding."

Her attention jerked down to her finger, and she wiped it again to her trousers before raising her eyes back to the man who was no man. War stood entirely too close to her, and she had no choice but to shrink back in her seat, covered entirely by his towering shadow. He went down to a knee before her and pulled a strip off his long dark shirt made of a material she'd never touched or seen before. Entirely too clean to belong in a place such as the one they were in.

"Your hand," he said.

For some reason, she extended her hand to him even though she'd rarely ever seen a nurse or had ever nursed a wound. She'd always let them be. If they festered and killed her, she would have been fine with it. The luck had it that they'd never did.

"For someone who bleeds so easily and so heavily, I'm surprised to know that you're my earnest soldier."

Rowan's hand jerked back, away from him, as if she'd been whipped. And that earned her his attention again. The violet in his irises looked turbulent. "You," she breathed.

Him.

Only heard of.

Never seen.

She'd prayed hard to never have that chance.

He raised a brow. "Me?"

Immediately, she shot up to her feet and made to move away, only to be blocked by the table behind her.

He stood, too, towering over her again. "They say a God has sway over their most benevolent admirer. So why is it that my sway fades with you even though you've been following my orders most ardently? Why is it that I have so little sway over you when you've led and won so many wars in my name?"

"In your name?" she asked, astounded by his statement.

"Every war is led in my name. You've led many of them."

That angered her—enraged her cold blood and filled it with fire. "Maybe I hoped that the next one I fought would end in your demise."

"There is no hope in war, Rowan. If you wish to deceive me somehow, you'd achieve greater results using less of that word." He wrapped a hand around her wrist and put the blade back in her hand before pulling the sharp edge to his throat. "My demise is also my victory. There is no war without demise. No win caused by no demise. No loss caused by no demise. My existence finds no end in demise. A win or a loss, all is victory to me. If it is my end you wish to find, I'd try something else."

"Maybe then I will take the easy way out. Maybe I will kill you."

"Might be a hard task for you."

"Not at all."

"Yet, we've been at these odds for over a minute and the only blood that has been spilled is yours."

"You think I would not take the chance?" Rowan asked, tightening her grip on the knife, and pushing the blade against his neck.

"One so determined would surely ask less questions."

When the clock kept ticking past seconds and then long minutes, he let go of her hand holding the blade and reached for the other that was still bleeding, carefully wrapping the fabric around the finger—because she'd let him. "You've never killed, have you, little thief?"

She scoffed, dropping the knife to the table, and pulling her other hand away from his. "I have," she gritted out, unwrapping the bandage, and throwing it back at him.

"But you've never taken a life with those hands."

"There are countless other ways to win wars."

"I'd like to hear every single one of them if you will allow me."

"Shouldn't you already know them all?"

"I do, but I like hearing you talk."

Rowan's hand reached back for the dagger on the table, fast enough to catch him by surprise, but not fast enough to injure him.

He leaned back, avoiding her attack. "Shouldn't we at least exchange first names, age, and occupation before jumping into such a relationship?"

Rowan didn't hesitate, she pushed to her feet, spinning fast and aiming the dagger right to his heart.

His hand wrapped around her wrist before she could pierce his skin. "My name is Elijah. Thought you might want to know before you try again."

"I don't give a damn," she hissed, dropping the dagger, and catching it under with her free hand, aiming at his stomach. Only for her other hand to end trapped in his grip, too.

"You give a little damn," he said, holding her there in a steel grip. "When you bury me like you buried the rest of your enemies, say it. I want you to say my name." His eyes dropped to her lips. "I want you to be the very last one to do so."

Rowan felt the chill of his words down her every bone. She groaned, struggling, and thrashing to get herself free. So unlike all the principles she'd been adhering to since a little child. There weren't supposed to be emotions when she fought. Her mind usually went blank in battle, utterly detached from the rest of her body. She never fought with anger or hunger. It helped her save energy, it helped her become resilient, and gave her more endurance than any other soldier. By the end of any battle, she was ready to start another while everyone else dragged their feet through exhaustion.

Focusing on her breathing, she emptied her mind again, her body going slack and unresisting. War thrived on anger, and she refused to see him feed from her own.

"Don't do that," he said, tilting his head to the side and smirking. "Don't talk yourself out of feeling angry when you are."

"Don't tell me what to do."

"For someone who takes orders so vehemently, that's an odd change of heart." He pulled at her hand, pressing the tip of her dagger right against his chest, the tip of the blade digging through his thin black shirt. "Are you ready to know what would happen if there was no war? Would you be able to face the consequences of my death?"

"With pleasure," she sneered, holding his gaze.

His grip on her hands loosened. "Then go ahead. Rid every world of war. Let them stand still. Let them be hit by famine and disease and remain still, indifferent. Let there be chaos while they stand still."

"War is chaos, too. Worse than chaos."

"War is order."

"Look no further than outside. Do you see order?"

"To be ambitious is not a crime."

"Murder is."

"Death is inevitable. If not by war, it will be by something else. Die in battle, or die starving, begging, retching, ridden with disease." He stepped closer to her. "You believe man would not kill man if there was no desire for war? It is human nature to be malicious. I only use it to my advantage, I do not give them their nature. Humanity is born with it."

"You encourage it."

"Nonsense. I've never done such a thing."

"Lies."

He scowled, almost offended at her accusation. "I am a God. I don't bother myself with such human manners."

Rowan's grip on the blade loosened just slightly. She blamed it on the sweat coating her palm. Then on the little cut on her finger. She blamed it on everything.

"What?" he asked. "Saddened to hear the truth?"

"Disappointed."

"So you believe me?"

She did. Part because she knew Gods didn't lie. Part because it wasn't hard to believe the truth he'd just spoken of. Rowan had never been afraid of Gods, but she'd been afraid of men. Because she'd seen them do worse harm than any God had ever done. "Did you lie?"

"No."

"And can you do that math or is it too hard for your godly mind?"

"And she jokes."

"Choke on your laughter while you're at it."

"What an awful way to die."

She scoffed. Almost laughed, too, but she was rather aggravated. "You've never been on a battlefield, have you, oh mighty God of War? You would have seen a thousand more ugly ways to die there."

"I've seen all of them, every single war there has been fought, and I will be here to see the very last one. To die on the battlefield—to die by a blade is an honour." He leaned in, bending down to her a little so their faces were close. "So don't back down on me now. Finish what you started."

He would be her first kill and watch him bleed until his very last breath, Rowan was sure of it. "In a minute," she said, spinning and throwing her dagger through the thin fabric tent wall.

A small groan let her know she'd hit the target. And she headed outside to find the intruder who'd sneaked inside their camp. A boy no more than fifteen had dropped to the muddy ground, nursing an injured leg, and moaning in pain.

"Don't pull the dagger out unless you wish to die," Rowan jadedly warned, slowly approaching him.

The young spy tried to scurry away, but stopped when Rowan didn't move from where she stood and raised an impatient brow at him instead. "What are you going to do with me?"

"What were you going to do with what you've gathered in our camp?"

He pressed his lips together, starting to shake from the blood loss and the sudden realisation of what he'd done. "They were going to send my little brother or someone else's brother, son, daughter. No one cares anymore."

"But you care. You cared enough to take your brother's place and give yourself a death sentence."

He started violently shaking at Rowan's last words, but managed a nod. "If it is meant to be so, then it cannot be changed."

"This is where you're supposed to beg," Rowan said, kneeling down to the boy and inspecting the wound she'd inflicted on him. "Did no one teach you to beg for your life first?"

"What good will it do?"

"I could be remorseful."

"You're General Rowan of Ingburn," he said, wincing as Rowan tightly tied a piece of her own bandage above the wound. "You have no soul. They say your parents sold it in exchange for your war skills."

"Untrue," she said, wedging the blade out of his leg. "They sold it for a sack of potatoes. Then the merchant who bought me sold me to the barracks once they figured I wasn't a boy."

"That is horrible."

"Also very untrue. My parents loved me."

The boy blinked fast. "O-oh."

"Also a lie. See what I did there?" She stayed there, pressing on his wound, thinking how her parents never had that chance—to love her. "It is easy to believe lies. Even easier to tell them."

After thinking for a minute, he asked, "You...you want me to lie to them?"

"Whether you lie to them or tell them the truth about what you saw or heard today will bear no significance in this war. You counted the thousands of armouries we have that you do not have. You noted the thousands of soldiers we have that you do not have. You saw our strategies that you have no chance of evading. Whether you tell them our numbers or strategies, whether you fight us knowing them or not, you will lose. Fighting with the knowledge you are going to lose will not give them much spirit to fight. Your men are owed at least that—they're owed hope. If they step on that battlefield without hope, they've already died once. It is your choice to spare them an extra death." Tying one last extra knot to make sure it would not come loose enough to let him lose more blood on the way back to his village, Rowan helped him to his uninjured foot.

His chin trembled and stray tears streamed down his dirt smeared cheeks. "We're all going to die, aren't we? My brother, too?"

Tilting her face up to the burning skies that had suddenly spared them some sunshine after bitter rain, she closed her eyes. "I already killed you, didn't I?"

The boy's hoarse sobs shook the very ground Rowan stepped on as she helped him to the edge of her camp and onto the concealed path that would take him back to his town.

Rowan couldn't force herself to return to camp. She stayed there, watching the boy she'd killed disappear through the forest, wondering how many souls she'd taken without making them bleed at all. That was her power. That was her gift from the God who'd tempted her enough to feel anger for the first time in a long while. Rowan's magic was human in all ways even though she never even partly felt human at all. Rowan knew how to dissect the human mind, how to numb it with fear, how to terrorise it with hopelessness. It was how she'd come this far into the life she had not wanted, thriving in it, too. Her strategies had never touched a human body, only their mind. She'd drowned lands to scare people into thinking of storms and flee instead of fight, she dried lakes and rivers into scarcity and hunger. She planted lies here, there, and everywhere human words could seed. And lies were like weed, they took everywhere, even in the most barren of soils. She'd robbed soil out of iron, depriving them of weaponry. She had hunted for food no one needed just so she could taunt her enemy into starvation. And that was how Rowan killed. Without touching blood, without seeing life seep out of anyone's eyes, without hearing a single last breath.

"You're a merciless little creature," the cold, dark voice of War cooed in her ear. "You should have just killed him and spared the boy some misery."

And despite his heavy presence behind her, she did not turn, she let him linger there. Heart pacing fast, thinking of what he'd do to her. Hoping it would be something unmerciful.

Rowan had only ever wanted one thing. She wanted whoever was writing her story to end it. Because she couldn't.

Rowan was hoping.

Rowan finally had hope.

That maybe he would do it.

That the God of War would be the one to do so. The one who had already killed her once long ago, when he'd robbed her of the desire to live.

"Maybe he won't die, after all," she said, turning to him even though he was closer to her than she'd thought. "Maybe you will die first."

"Fingers crossed."

"Fingers crossed," Rowan agreed, playing to his tune just to see if it aggravated him the same as it aggravated her. Unluckily for her, it looked like he enjoyed blowing his own horn because

WENDY HEISS

he grinned down at her. "Do you enjoy suffering this much?"

"Immensely. I wouldn't be the God of War if I didn't."

"You're right, you'd just be the God of Morons."

"Maybe you meant belligerence."

"No, I meant morons. Take away the psychopathy and lack of empathy, and you're just a moron."

"Perhaps I am."

"Since it is a moment of realisation, maybe you can reflect on other things."

"Such as?"

"The reasons for the moronity."

"I'll try."

Rowan rolled her eyes and stepped to leave, but Elijah moved in front of her again. "Yes?"

He blinked. "Nothing else?"

She blinked back. "When I'll think of something else, I will make it known."

"Please do."

Utterly confused, Rowan took one slow step back and then another, until she was at a distance where she could make a run for it. She was itching to make a run for it, but she forced her burning feet to calmly and inconspicuously take gentle, unfearful steps away from him.

War chuckled. "I'm not going to jump on you, Rowan. You'll trip walking backwards all the way to the camp."

Her steps slowed, turned lingering and languid. "Why did you show yourself in this realm?"

"Hard to hate such a handsome face, isn't it?" He cleared his throat. "Don't answer that. I'm sure whatever you will say will hurt my feelings."

"Strange how a simple mirror hasn't done that already."

He closed his eyes and smiled. "Whew, that stung."

"Why won't you answer me?"

"I want you to keep talking to me. Everyone else will either bow to lick my boots or stare at me until I get a headache. Just not you. I like how you talk to me."

She had the sudden urge to pick up a rock and bash his handsome head in. Instead, she spun to leave, halting only when he called to her. "Fine, fine." He pointed for her to sit on a wooden log. "It's a long story."

"I'm sure you can shorten it."

"I don't really want to."

Crossing her arms over her chest, she remained standing while he sat by a boulder. "I was hoping someone I know would have made it out of this war," he said, making Rowan frown impossibly hard. "She didn't though."

"A human?"

He nodded. "A human."

"You'd told Daniel something else."

"Is he your lover?"

Rowan choked on an inhale and sputtered a breathless laughter.

And that seemed enough of an answer to him because he nodded, even smiled, too. "I told him the truth. I also came to witness the last battle before the end of the war in this realm."

"Why?"

"Because it is something that has never happened before. Wars never come to an end."

"That means you will leave this realm alone?"

"You really believe it is I who has not left this realm alone?" He cocked an eyebrow up. "They pray for me, Rowan. Not to me. They do not pray to me to let them be. They wish for me, they yearn for me, they seek my blessing." For a quiet moment, he just looked at her—something that flustered her because no one had ever looked at her, not like he was—in fact, no one really dared to look at Rowan at all, let alone like that. They didn't dare say her name as he did either. "It is strange how you've been surrounded all your life with people who have prayed for me and never have noticed it. Not all do, but most have. Usually, the ones that never have are the ones who have lost hope entirely, those that fight because there either is nothing for them to do or because they know of nothing else."

"How do you not hate it?"

"Do you hate what you are?"

Rowan didn't hesitate. "Yes."

She didn't know why the look in his eyes softened, or why the violet in his eyes turned such a pale lilac. "Why?"

It was the easiest and simplest thing Rowan had ever answered. "Because the world would be so much better if I didn't exist."

He looked away from her for the first time since they'd met, his gaze rising to the dull, waning moon. "You do not know how untrue that is."

"I do not need your flattery," she bitterly snapped, feeling a deep seated anger limber up. "You still haven't answered me."

"I'm not ready for you to stop talking just yet."

Rowan's patience had it for the night. And turning round, she walked towards the forest. Without her answer. Only with more questions.

Three poppies

SHE'D LIED.

She'd sat at their meeting, all eyes and attention on her, and she had lied to all of them.

When the other two generals had asked her for the layout plans of the last battle ahead before they would take the Gobresh capitol, she'd lied.

The river tide, she had told them.

Not in their favour for crossing any time soon.

Even the detailed calculations she'd taken and mapped out for them were all false. Elijah knew that because he'd seen her take those measurements and written the wrong numbers down intentionally. He'd followed her around all day, watching her do what he was told was the best anyone could do, and she'd done the exact opposite. Instead of letting them know that it was the most favourable time to cross the largest river between the kingdoms, she'd made them wait for another moon.

She'd made him a liar, too.

As when the generals and the captains had glanced at him for approval, he'd remained silent. And that had been enough of a confirmation to them.

There was only one intention behind it that sounded somewhat sane to Elijah. She wanted to delay them. The reasoning for that, however, he could not think of.

"They fell for your lies unusually fast," he said, taking a seat beside her as General Adam and the rest left the tent.

Her movement halted and she froze entirely. There was nothing on her face to let anyone know that she was affected in any way by him knowing the truth as she looked up at him. "They did. I've done nothing for them to doubt my words. I've won them countless battles," she easily confessed to him, making him doubt every single thing he'd known about her so far.

"But you don't want to win this one for them?"

She returned to her papers, rolling them neatly and placing them back in her bag. Not answering him.

"You could lie to me," he probed, wanting her to keep talking to him.

"What would the point be?"

"What if I tell them?" He wouldn't. He wasn't there to meddle in human affairs. Especially not with such interesting ones that Rowan was wanting to twist.

She scoffed, and it was the closest thing to amusement he'd seen from her. "Then tell them."

"You don't fear repercussions?"

With a sigh, she spun to him, and a feigned stunned expression was etched in her features, something so entirely not her. Something that took him by surprise and confused him. "I...I am really sorry, Adam," she snivelled, her eyes rounding and widening with false fear. "I...I didn't think...didn't know I'd calculated them wrong. There must be something wrong. I really didn't mean to do it."

When he smiled up at her, the mask she'd just put on melted off her face, bringing back the bored and lifeless look she always wore. He slowly clapped, chuckling. "Fascinating." Shaking his head, he said, "Frailty does not suit you, though. I've never known a woman to be frail."

"That is strange because frailty is all men see when they look at a woman. Whether it suits us or not."

"Men have strange eyes. They never usually connect to their brains."

She spared him a glance. "Thankfully for me."

"Unfortunately for them." He leaned forward, resting his elbows on his knees as he studied her. "Why are you delaying them?"

"Who says I am trying to delay them?"

"Then what are you trying to do? Get yourself caught and be killed as a traitor to your queen?"

"Perhaps."

"A dishonourable death your kind would say."

"There is no honour in death. Whoever thinks otherwise simply is afraid of death."

"And you aren't?"

"Why would I be afraid of liberation? Look around. Life here feels like you're living in your own land under enemy rule. You're either a survivor or a slave."

She left before Elijah could ask her what she was. If she was a survivor or a slave. But maybe he knew. He could tell from her eyes that she'd not survived. That her soul still clung to this world somehow, made a slave to serve soulless men.

The boy, Daniel, sat near her at the dinner area, laughing and gabbling at her. Though she didn't engage with him at all, she didn't bark rude remarks or send scathing glares in his direction like she did to most—like she did to him. Instead, she let him go on and on and on about ridiculous things that didn't need such attention.

Elijah got to his feet when the boy threw an arm over her stiff shoulders. And that was enough to draw Rowan's attention in his direction. The glaring returned, and Elijah couldn't help himself from chuckling.

He threw her a wink, and she almost recoiled, wincing and cringing and shaking her head at him. Only a gag would have completed the look of utter disgust she flashed at him.

He wondered if he'd always been this masochistic because he enjoyed that reaction far too much.

When she joined the rest of the soldiers to leave the designated open dining space, he stepped before her. She was a tall woman, but he still threw shade over her entire body. And even her eyes, the green in them turning almost black when she tipped her head back to look at him. "Any particular reason why you aggravate me on purpose?"

"What did I do?"

"Breathe."

"Apologies for insulting you as such, but with great pain I have to tell you that unless you kill me, I will keep doing so."

Her eye twitched and she made to step away, but he blocked her path again. "What?" she snapped at him.

"I just wanted to see."

"See what?"

"You and your angry eyes. Closely."

"Gods give me strength," she murmured low between her teeth.

"Pray to me and I'll give you all the strength there is. After all, you're part of this," he said, gesturing around the camp. "How can you not?"

"It's because of those who have prayed for you that I am here."

"Why not choose to remain away from it?"

"You think I was even given a choice when they burned my family home, killed my parents, and sold me to this cause?"

Elijah took a painful moment to gather an answer. "I can give the choice back to you. To leave all of this behind."

"You don't understand, do you?"

"Make me."

"How is that my job? Do your eyes not suffice to see the bed that was made for me? What a luxury would it be to leave this behind. To be able to close my eyes and not see what I've been seeing for the past fifteen years. What a luxury to be able to pretend I've not committed the sins I was forced to commit. To not remember the choices that I've had to make. Choices of forcing children to be slaughtered in their own homes, asleep. Or awake, facing the blade of a blood-hungry soldier who will not stop at their death." She took a deep breath. "Do not tell me what humanity is and is not. How it heeds and prays to you. How none of this falls in your hands because you simply grant what you've been asked of. Because I know. But do not ridicule me with your offers. Being here is a big enough sin. I am not ready to commit the sin of closing my eyes before catastrophe. I will bear witness even if it consumes me whole. I will remember every face, every name, and repent for all of it. If I am forced to be here, it is the least I can do. Being consumed by guilt is the way I wish to die if I am ever granted the honour of leaving this wretched world."

He was wrong to assume that it was anger he was seeing in her eyes. Desolation often looked like resentment, condemnation. "Forgive me."

Rowan's eyes widened for a moment. "For what?"

"You asked me if I hated what I was. Maybe I do."

She still wasn't convinced if she'd heard what he'd told her correctly. After all, why would the God of War condemn what he was? Why would he even apologise to her?

The greatest question out of all was the strange interest he'd taken on her particularly. She'd not seen him speak a single word to anyone else or even reply to anything that he was asked by curious and infatuated soldiers who'd done nothing by marvel and awe at the sight of him. Even though he'd sat in on every meeting they'd had, watched every training session, and heard every single plan made, she was almost entirely sure he'd not paid mind to a single thing that was told or shown.

Despite his presence, he'd shown so little interest in this war that she was beginning to wonder if there was even a point to him being among them. She wondered if he couldn't make himself leave after he'd found out the human he'd sought was dead. Maybe he was lingering because he was hopeless and grieved his findings. But she quickly shook her thoughts when she remembered that despite his human form, he wasn't human at all.

Even from afar, she could tell she was being watched. Bent low near the river bank, she studied the stream and the clear crystal water of the longest and largest river in Tisiania that separated the north and south. Mugril and Gobresh. Well, part of Gobresh. Part of Gobresh above it was now claimed as Mugril land.

His voice came from behind her before she felt him there, "There is rain coming."

One glance at the skies and you could tell that rain had no such desire. "You can predict the weather now?" she asked, keeping her back to him as she scribbled down useless notes in her diary which she knew Henry's and Adam's soldiers checked daily when she left her tent.

"There is wind, and where there is wind there is rain. I thought you'd know this much since they hold you in such high regard for knowing humans and nature very ably. I'm told you use it to your favour all the time, to aid this army and its invasions. To know how to make nature your ally is not easy. Nature does not make allies, and it usually has a mind of its own when it comes to choosing sides and who to favour."

"They've been lucky guesses," she confessed. They'd actually been desperate guesses that had somehow turned true. Sometimes to her dismay because they'd worked too well. Well enough to convince just about everyone she was vital to this war.

"No such thing as lucky guesses. If nature has favoured you when you wished for its help, then it's simply a game of convincing it of your intentions."

Rowan didn't wish to entertain him, didn't wish to regard him, nor acknowledge him at all. But she found herself doing the opposite. "You regard nature as an entity?"

"Because it is. One body. Soil is its skin. The trees are its lungs. The rivers, the lakes, and the seas are its blood. And humans are tiny little parasites who give an unbearable itch you can never get rid of."

Her eyes drew shut when she felt the urge to laugh. And then she ran a hand over her disobeying features until they schooled back to normal before turning to him. "Now we are parasites."

"A harmless metaphor."

"Metaphors are indirect ways of telling the truth."

"Didn't say it was a harmless lie."

Her mouth twitched and she bit her lip hard until the metallic taste of blood soured her mouth. "Was the human you were looking for also one?"

"Because she meant something to me didn't make her anything special. On the contrary, it made her a target."

"Whose?"

"Fate's."

She frowned. "Aren't you the King of Gods? The bearer of *Dawnbringer*?"

"There is always something that stands above us, Rowan. And something that stands above them, and so forth. We aren't masters of our own fate. We're simply slaves without shackles. I might have power over you, but there are things that have power over me. It is how it will always be."

She could understand though she would have preferred it not

to. She didn't wish to understand a God like him. "You don't seem interested in our war."

"I've seen too many of them to find any interest in them anymore."

"Why did you apologise to me the other day?"

His head tilted to the side. "You have so many questions, Rowan of Ingburn. How do they ever sate your curiosity around here?"

"By answering me."

He flashed her a slow smile as he backed away to sit on a raised rock, not far from her. "I was born in a fire. Fleshed from smoke and flames. That is how they tell my story. I am not like the rest of Gods, born in their power, born from necessity. My existence does not predate humanity. I was born along with humanity though I am far from being human. When you are what I am, it is sometimes impossible to acknowledge the consequences of my birth. To question my existence. I am simply a derivative of hate, anger, greed, desire." The strange God looked away from her to stare at the loud stream of water. "Once you become accustomed to your own scent, you slowly start to forget it is even there."

For a brief second, she could almost relate to him. "Then why did you apologise?"

His attention flustered her, but she forced her strained neck to keep still when his violet gaze returned to hers. Under the sun, it was such a pale violet, so soft, so gentle to belong to someone like him. "I might be the creation of others, a simple consequence, but I am also an entity. One who has simply ignored what I am. That is a choice. One the very few I am permitted to have. The least I can be for the harm that I have caused is regretful."

"If it is pity you are offering, I don't need it. And I highly doubt you need me to accept it."

"Believe me, Rowan. You'd know what my pity looks like." He stood and reached her closer, kneeling as she had, still forcing her to tilt her head back to look up at him because of the sheer size of him. "I don't need you to accept my apology either. I'd rather you not. I've grown intensely fond of the way you look at me. Unsure if it is to strangle me or eat me whole."

A vein on her temple pumped intensely hard and fast. "There is something terribly wrong with you."

"Well, isn't that true," he crooned, his eyes dropping all over her face, tracing the messy braid resting on her left shoulder, and further down her plain, borrowed loose clothes she wore.

The look he gave her was intense enough that she subconsciously looked down at herself, wondering if her shirt that surely had been white once had any stains in it. "So help me Gods," she mumbled low between her teeth as she chastised herself for even caring.

"What do you want me to help you with that you so desperately call upon me?" he asked, smirking at her.

"I didn't call upon you."

"You think any other God heard you speaking that low?"

She stood and glared down at him who was now looking up at her as if she was some sort of a shrine, violet eyes eating her whole. Rowan had never been looked at like that. Like she was something to behold. It made her uneasy to think why he would regard her as such. It made her wonder if she was being made an accessory to some evil plan of his. But then, she was sure he could knit evil plans all on his own.

"Yes?" he asked, remaining kneeling right before her.

"I don't know what this sick and twisted fascination that you have for me is."

"I might be sick and twisted, but believe me, my fascination with you isn't."

"Hard to believe."

"Then I will have to be more convincing."

Four poppies

ROWAN HAD GONE OVER every map, every historical detail, every number from population to streets and shops. They were one battle away from winning the war.

One last battle.

They could march there tomorrow and win it, but no one knew that beside her.

Everyone had already started making plans on what they would do after it.

Rowan had tried to do the same. But there were no plans she could think of. She had no loved one to return to. No home. No city she could call hers. The one she'd been born in no longer existed. Destroyed in the battle that took her parents away and almost had her captured by Mugril slavers. Mugril, not Gobresh. Her own people would have sold her less than what five pounds of poultry cost.

She grabbed a hairbrush that an old kitchen maid had given her fifteen years ago that first night when she'd shown up at her door looking less like a human and more like something that belonged in a barn. She'd taken pity on Rowan. Bathed her and then combed her hair—it was the most anyone had done for her in her whole entire life. Even left her the comb to keep. It was the only item she'd held onto. Nothing else belonged to her. Only that one comb.

Pulling at the hair tie, she undid her braid and then violently had a go at her hair, trying to comb out the tangles from the thick curls and the frizzy strands. No one had taught her how to do it properly. Most men kept their hair short, and the only women who had joined the soldier ranks kept their hair short as well, sometimes shaved, too. Despite never having loved her hair, never having been attached to it, Rowan refused to cut it, let alone shave it. It was the one thing that heavily distinguished her from the other soldiers, and she liked them knowing that they were taking orders from a woman.

A distant scream made her put the comb down and head straight outside, her long frizzy hair blowing everywhere in the night wind as she searched for the owner of the harrowing call.

Three men had surrounded a girl, laughing and picking at her clothes, hooting and cackling the more she cried. The girl was Gobresh. Rowan could tell the language she was begging in. It was so different from any other spoken in Tisiania, and it was the hardest one she'd learnt. When she realised the soldiers had gone into a nearby town without permission and very much so against her orders, not only putting them at risk of being captured and tortured for information but had stolen what she'd explicitly demanded they stay away from, Rowan felt a desire that had long slept inside her. She felt rage.

"What do you think you are doing?" she asked, surprisingly calm despite the simmer in her blood. She knew the men had recognised her voice without even looking at her because their bodies went rigid.

All three turned to her at once, directing a drunken look down at her, one full of disregard.

The war was ending. Soon, they'd be rid of the general who'd allowed no such thing as what they were about to do. It was the condition Rowan had demanded when the two older generals had requested she join their ranks. Women were not to be touched. Children were not to be touched.

"She came willingly," one soldier foolishly said.

Rowan's gaze slid to the girl, and she asked in her tongue, "Did you join them willingly?"

"No, no, I didn't, they came inside my home, hurt my father and mother, and stole me away," the girl hurriedly said, and the men all let out a sound of annoyance, surely realising they'd made a mistake.

Rowan didn't like mistakes, nor did she make them. She was particularly meticulous and hated loose ends. And the only way she fixed loose ends was by burning them.

Again, foolishly, one of them approached her—approached her too closely, more closely than they normally had the courage to. "Walk away."

Rowan tilted her head back and stared up at his empty eyes that were somehow so vibrant with life—unlike hers. The blue was dirtied, just like his soul. "I've not had entertainment for myself in a long while." She turned to look at the Gobresh girl. "Hand this one to me. Play with her after I am done."

The soldier looked taken aback. Then he barked an uncomfortable laughter which his two friends followed. "You want her?" he asked, surprise colouring his tone.

"I want her."

He let out another rumbling laughter and patted her shoulder, hard enough to make the still open wound from the last battle scream and beg in agony. "Then have her tonight. But tomorrow she shall be ours."

"Tomorrow," Rowan said, extending a hand to the girl which she took almost immediately, flying into her arms like she was a shelter of sorts.

The soldiers left, howling, and laughing through their drunkenness, and Rowan dragged the girl to a storage tent, handing her a shovel.

"Dig," Rowan told her, pointing to the free patch of land by the tents.

Eyes wide and confused, the girl took a few steps away and began digging through the muddy ground without asking a single question.

Rowan's fingers and arms felt like they were going to fall off any minute, but she kept going until there were three deep holes dug. Humans underestimated the sheer force of spite.

There was a sudden pause in Rowan's digging, and she looked up, searching the surrounding forest as if a beast was about to prowl in her direction. Her senses were honed, sharpened by experience, she knew there was something hiding behind the darkness of the trees—something malicious.

There was no beast, however.

There was a God who prowled in her direction. All entertained and amused, Elijah sat at the edge of one of the holes she'd dug. "Looks cosy."

"How about you give it a try?"

He leaned back on his elbows as if he was sunbathing, and grinned up at the dark, starless skies that desperately held onto a pale crescent moon. "My last wish is to be burned."

"That would be a waste of a fire," Rowan said, still not realising where her courage to talk to a God like him even came from. Despite what she was, she wasn't entirely fearless. On the contrary, Rowan was more of a coward than one would realise.

War threw his head back and laughed. "You should've just gutted them."

"I don't *gut*."

He stretched wide, letting out a small groan. "What plan do we have for them?"

She paused, rolling her tired eyes up at him. "*We*?"

He pointed between the Gobresh girl, himself, and then at Rowan. "I like group activities."

"Get in the hole," Rowan said, dropping her shovel. "You might like this group activity."

"A kind offer." He stood, looking down at where she'd sunk inside the hole, and offered a hand to her. "It's deep enough now."

For some reason, his eyes haunted her enough to say, "I don't want sunlight to ever reach their bodies."

"It won't. Come out now, Rowan."

Entranced by that beckoning, she climbed out of the hole without his aid, and then helped the Gobresh girl out of hers. "I'll walk you home," Rowan told her.

The girl nodded, clinging to Rowan's arm. And Rowan sighed, wondering if the girl even realised who or what she was holding, that she'd been the main cause for her people's demise.

Beside the sound of owls and the cicadas that had made themselves visible after the rain, there was something else getting on her nerves and patience that she'd tried so hard to master.

"Don't you have something else to do?" she asked, glowering at the God of War who'd followed after them.

"Nice of you to worry, but no, I don't."

"No one's pain to sit back and laugh at?" she spat.

"None that I can think of."

Rowan halted and spun to him, almost taking the God of War by surprise. "Go away."

"Your hair is down."

"What?"

"You're only wearing a shirt, no armour, the only weapon you had was the shovel and you've left that behind. There could be rebels lingering by, wild animals, or the men you sent off might have realised you've tricked them."

"And that concerns you why?"

He blinked. "Uncertain."

"Go be uncertain somewhere else."

"Are you ordering me, Rowan?"

"What if I am?"

"I am a God."

"I do not care."

"That I see."

"Go annoy someone else."

His brows jumped up at that. "I'm happy to annoy *you*. Might even tell you a little story on our way to take this lovely young lady *safely* home."

She spun and grabbed the girl, pulling her faster towards the forest. "I don't want to hear your damn story."

"Then maybe the forest would like to hear it. Nature loves this story I am about to tell. It always weeps."

"For you to stop maybe."

"Well, perhaps," he agreed, to her chagrin, matching her quick steps with too much ease. "There once was—"

"Oh, unholy Gods," she murmured, and he laughed, making all of Rowan's thoughts pause for a minute. They'd never done that before. Rowan was always thinking. She couldn't even remember a moment when she'd not been thinking.

"There once was a boy and a girl who stood at the edge of the world watching the sun rise north."

"There is no such thing," Rowan sighed.

"It's a story, little thief. So, if the story says there once was, then there once had been," he said, and then continued, "A long time ago when there was no order. When the sun rose from the north and fell south. When stars shone day and night. When day was young, and night was old. Right when all the Gods were born. What they call the dawn of time. The boy and the girl met then, watching it all unfold before their eyes. He was *turmoil* and she was *tranquil*. And as they watched the sun rise east for the first time," he said, reaching for Rowan's hair to pluck a leaf from the thick curls that were still loose, "they made a vow to one another. They'd only be apart when the sun would no longer set west, when day would once again become old, and the stars would never cease to shine. When the Gods that were born would be unborn." There was a pause in his words, and Rowan found herself almost curious enough to ask him to continue. "The boy and the girl had been heard by the new Gods who'd risen with more than just desire for power. They'd risen with greed, with hunger. They did not like the fact that where there was *turmoil* there would always be *tranquil*. They didn't like the balance of things. They'd decided that only they could place order amongst the realms."

"Why?" Rowan asked despite herself. Suddenly curious about his stupid little tale that made no sense at all. But then, she'd found him to be a nonsensical God entirely.

"Because the order of things comes from disorder. How could they place it when there was already an order? It went against the need they'd been born from."

"That's ridiculous."

"So thought *tranquil* and *turmoil*. Then the Gods found a way to part them from one another despite the unbreakable bargain they had made. They made him a God. Then they made him King of the Gods once they realised humanity craved what he was."

Rowan stopped walking, and so did the girl and War, both looking at her with a curious expression on their moonlit faces that were half covered by night. "Why would they do that?" she asked. "Why wouldn't they make *her* Queen of the Gods instead?"

"Because an eternity of turmoil would mean an eternity of their rule. An eternity for them to maintain balance. And an eternity of tranquil would have rendered them useless. If everything stood still and peaceful, then a new order of life and death would have been established. No need for anything else. No matter how much I dislike the bastard, *Death* would have made a great King of All," he said, lifting his eyes to the moon and letting Rowan watch the colour of his irises turn a light shade of lilac. "At least he wouldn't have made her what they did."

For some reason, Rowan was almost afraid to ask what she asked next, "And what did they make her?"

He finally looked back at her. He looked at her as if he'd looked at her for years, decades, perhaps eternity. A look so familiar and filled with such longing, such desperation. "They made her small."

"Small?" she asked, her voice low, almost a whisper.

Elijah nodded. "They rid her with an illness made entirely of loathing and spite. Then they banished her to live among humankind. To watch them suffer. To grow even smaller under their suffering which she couldn't help anymore. Unlike him, she was no longer immortal. Reborn as someone else in every lifetime."

"And the bargain they made? The promise they made to one another?"

The God of War smiled down at her. "You paid attention."

"Answer me."

"It turned into a curse. He'd look for her in every lifetime and he'd find her. *Turmoil* would find her only after she died. They say peace dies last. But she never died last for him. She always died first when he was near her. So, he only looked from afar, and she never even knew."

"And?"

"And what?"

"The ending. What's the ending? All stories have endings."

"Not this one."

"Nonsense."

His head tilted to the side and his smile grew into a grin. "You think so, little thief?"

Rowan rolled her eyes and grabbed the girl, dragging her towards the town faster. "You're done annoying me, I suppose."

"Not truly. But it's fascinating watching you think so hard. I didn't want to interfere with whatever thought you're dissecting so intently. Wouldn't wish to be caught between that blade."

She cast him a quick glance. "Why me out of all that you can pester in this realm?"

"Indeed, why you?"

"Just answer me."

"You remind me of someone I knew long ago."

"*Tranquil*, as you called her."

He stopped walking, and with a sigh, she stopped walking, too. Refusing to turn to him just yet. She was waiting for him to answer as she was terribly afraid that she'd been correct.

"Yes," he admitted, just as she had thought.

"And you're *turmoil*."

"Was," he said. "A long time ago. Somewhere between night and day, I became *War*."

"What about her? What did she become?"

"The air I needed to breathe."

Rowan turned to him then, needing to see him when she would say, "I'm not her."

The violent violet of his eyes calmed, softened, turned molten. "No, you're not."

It was nothing Rowan had imagined. She'd expected realisation or perhaps even distraught, but what was left there in his too soft of a gaze was only melancholy. "Then leave me be."

He was looking at her so softly. "Even to someone like me, it would be such a cruel thing to ask. I haven't seen her in so long. I haven't breathed in so long."

"I'm not her," Rowan repeated, her heart beating out of her chest. For a very brief moment, she had wanted to be her just so she could taste what it felt to be wanted, needed, grieved. For she'd already inherited the same rotten fate as his lover.

"Let a man starved of air think he can breathe."

She turned away, not bearing the look in his eyes anymore. A look that wasn't meant for her.

Rowan had never been looked at like that. Like she was vital. She wanted to loathe her, to loathe the woman who had that power over someone like him. She couldn't though. Because how could she loathe a woman who'd made a cruel man like him look so utterly pitiful when he talked about her.

For a moment, Rowan wanted to look back at him. She wanted to know how it felt to be looked at as if she was the most difficult thing someone has lost. But she was yet to give into her desperations.

After dropping the girl at the nearest point to the small Gobresh village she could reach without being noticed by any lingering soldier of the Gobresh King that might be hiding between the women and the elderly, she headed back, following the faint light of the northern star. It had taken everything in her not to linger and watch the villagers, to not count the children and their mothers, grandparents or even fathers if they had somehow escaped being drafted in the last battle they had lost.

Most of the Gobresh people had refused to leave or even evacuate the villages and cities despite the Mugril army eating through their lands, burning them, and claiming the ashes as their own. They'd chosen to die where they had been born.

Rowan had tried to learn how this war had all started nearly twenty-five years ago, yet none had been reason enough for her to justify the damage that had been done.

The Gobresh King and Mugril Queen had once been allies, friends.

Lovers, too.

There had been talk of joining Tisiania as one.

Talk of a union that had soon grown into talk of eradication.

One wanting to eat over the other.

One sudden summer afternoon, before day could blink into night, the war had started. One summer afternoon was all it had taken for the Mugril Queen to decide that Tisiania was hers by a right no one had granted her. One afternoon was all it had taken her to convince her court that the Mugril people were owed a right over the entirety of Tisiania. One afternoon was all it had taken for the Mugril to agree, to support her claim to the land, to support her order of banishment to the Gobresh people, to indoctrinate her people into believing their own lies, their own superiority already inflated by such terrible, terrible greed. One afternoon was all it had taken for young and old to join her armies. And then, one red morning stained with death, they'd raised the Mugril flag over the first Gobresh city.

"Why did you favour one over the other?" she asked, leaning over a bush to pick the ripe, maroon berries that had grown all over it, and filling her pockets. "Why make Mugril armies richer, bigger?"

"I have no such power over humanity, Rowan. Your queen's deepest desires have sought me and my blessing, while the Gobresh King prays to another."

"Who?" she asked, glancing over her shoulder, her hand frozen over a bush.

"A son of a bastard by the name of Gabriel. The one you all call the God of Life. Mugril mothers pray that their sons and daughters return victorious. While Gobresh mothers pray their sons and their daughters return alive. Not all, of course, but the majority overwhelms significantly. You can ask me why, but my answer is plain, and it might not satisfy your curiosity."

Abandoning the berry picking, she turned to him. "If we are so inherently bad, what worth is our existence? Why do we live—" She took a deep breath, and asked, "Why do we even exist? Is it to suffer, watch each other suffer, or make each other suffer? Who takes pleasure from it?" Rowan's eyes lifted to his. "You?"

"Though I am sure there are those who do watch suffering with eagerness, human existence cannot be defined by suffering."

"How can it not?" Her chest felt heavy with emotion all of the sudden. "How? It is all that we do. Even in peace, even in prosperity, even in happiness we suffer."

His eyes softened, and she hated the comfort they gave her. "To feel so deeply is something only a human heart can do. Whether it be suffering, hate, desire, anger. Humanity all feels it intensely. Humans don't only suffer. They cannot. Not when they can feel so much more than any creature ever can."

He reached to pick a berry from her hand, but she slapped it away, covering her palm full of berries with her other hand. "Rowan's berries," he said, lifting his hands up. "I got it."

Rowan pointed a finger all around the bushes. "All of them are mine. Never eat them."

"Never?"

"Promise me," she found herself saying.

"Promise?" he asked, tilting his head to the side, and studying her intently. "Fine. I promise."

"Why do you look at me like that? Like I hold some secret key to some secret realm?"

"You're fascinating."

She scoffed. Rowan was nothing but scars and smoke and made of memories no one wanted. She wasn't fascinating. Her mere insignificant existence had become wanted only when it served to harm. If she were to die tomorrow, no one would have accounted for her death as any loss. But perhaps as victory. "Because I dislike you?" she asked.

His lips twitched in amusement. "Dislike? I thought it was something along the lines of hate."

"I don't waste that much energy to hate something or someone. It is pointless. Hating you is absolutely pointless." She secured the berries in her pockets and pointed to the bushes again. "Don't touch any of them."

He raised a brow. "I gave you my promise."

She nodded. Not that his promises meant much anyway.

Five poppies

MURMURS FILLED THE DINING grounds that stretched for a mile with thin, wooden tables lined parallel to one another. The seats were so compacted against each other that the whole burble felt like one body of a voice.

From where he had sat, he could clearly see every raised head and pair of eyes turned in her direction while her own attention was lowered over her food plate and her gaze was faint and struggling to remain open, begging for sleep and distant.

Last night, her lantern had remained lit inside her tent until dawn had set in. He'd seen the silhouette of her shadow through the wall made of fabric, sitting at the edge of her mattress, not moving at all. Sleep had not been kind to her. But considering how she was, maybe she had not been kind to sleep. The thought almost made him laugh.

Elijah wondered what she had thought of so deeply all night long. He wondered if she'd also thought of what they'd talked about. He was envious of her thoughts. For being inside what nothing else could get inside of—her mind.

The fog over her tired soul snapped when someone stepped in front of her table.

The general, Adam, stood over her, a furious look in his eyes—one that prompted Elijah to abandon his spot under a tree shadow where he usually watched her from. "Tell me, Rowan," he demanded, "why did I find three of my soldiers laying in...graves?"

She gave her peer a bored look. Perhaps just a tired one. "Well, the chances would be that they are dead. Since they are laying in graves."

"You killed them?" Adam harshly questioned, lowering his voice as he threw uncomfortable glances at the rest of the soldiers who reluctantly returned to pretending they weren't paying attention to them.

"Why would you think so?"

"There were webcap mushrooms on their plates, Rowan. Webcaps!" he hissed. "The cook said you took the food trays to their tents."

"So? I did not feed them their food, Adam. They ate it with their own hands."

The older general shook his head. "You cannot do this." He leaned in closer to her, cautious so he wouldn't be heard by the rest of the soldiers. "It is not the time to do this, Rowan. You should have just reported to me whatever they did to earn your anger."

"I'm not sure what you wanted me to report to you," she said with feigned disinterest, dusting her hands and leaning back on her chair.

"You heard her," Elijah found himself saying, and meddling in human matters. He took a seat at the table, not far from her. "It was an unfortunate mistake. You'll not lose your war because you lost three soldiers, General."

Adam seemed astounded at his interference. Probably because so far, Elijah had not said a word to anyone else beside her and her young friend. The general glanced fast between her and him, and stuttered, "I-it is a matter of respect and o-obedience."

"Whose? Yours? Theirs? Hers?"

Adam's shoulders pulled back and he stood straight as if he'd been called to salute. "There are rules in war, as you must know, your holiness."

He almost winced at the way he was addressed. "On the contrary. There are no rules in war," Elijah replied. "And you at least have to be smart enough to not accept food from someone you have wronged or attempted to wrong. I'd say those soldiers did not have a very promising future as it was."

Elijah had her attention then, she lifted her wide eyes to him, and he shot her a faint wink that her superior missed amidst his attempt to find words for a reply.

"It does not justify taking their lives," was all Adam could come up with.

"Nor can you justify your war with the Gobresh. But that is how it is. War simply does not care. Death does not care at all. Many unjust things are done in the name of war. In my name." He grinned at the general who uncomfortably shifted a few steps back as if he'd snarled instead. "And as far as what Rowan did goes, it was entertaining. I'm very entertained. Aren't you glad?"

The general's mouth parted as he stared at War as if he'd grown another head. "I...I—" He glanced at Rowan first before replying, "Yes, well, I am glad if that is the case."

With that, he bowed at Elijah and left towards the tents as if his soles had caught on fire.

"I don't need you to defend me," Rowan sneered.

He picked her water cup and drank from it, thankful it had been only water not the piss coloured poison the rest consumed. "I didn't defend you. I defended my assets." Elijah couldn't help himself but say, "You just happen to be one of them."

Suddenly, she looked so well rested and energetic, ready to pounce over the small table between them. "I am not something you own."

His eyes flashed. "How can I greatly persuade you to reconsider?" he asked, leaning over the table, bringing their faces closer. "I treat what I own with utmost care."

She slapped his hand away when he reached to touch her face, making him chuckle. "So very violent," he crooned, his eyes dropping to her mouth.

"You haven't seen the half of it."

"Then show me."

She looked ahead at where Adam had been joined by the other general, and winced—possibly because the two had just witnessed her slapping the God of War. Her head lowered, breaking Elijah's streak of fun. "Go. Away," she gritted between her clenched teeth.

"Go where?" he asked, picking a piece from her bread, and she shot him a bewildered look. Elijah found out bread didn't taste like much either in this realm. And he also found himself curious to taste something else. He'd had some of her anger. He wanted some of her frustration now. Up until that moment, he had not realised how much he enjoyed being glared at.

"To hell for all I care."

"I already am in hell, Rowan." She was all the way across from him. Staring at him with so much hate. Hate, not just anger. How could the one who reminded him of his lost peace hate him? Especially when he needed his peace back.

"Well, enjoy your stay," she said, pushing up and leaving.

He resisted the desire to follow after her. An urge he'd never suppressed before. He wasn't a God who held himself back from getting what he wanted, but she wasn't a human who'd give herself up without a fight. Dropping his head back, he shut his eyes and murmured a silent curse. His ears itched, as if already feeling the ridicule of Gods at his misery.

Someone dropped on a chair near him, and he sat up straight, expecting the same pair of angry eyes to be looking back at him, not the big brown doe ones belonging to the boy she somehow tolerated better than him.

"Hi," Daniel casually said to him.

Hi?

Elijah leaned forward, not wanting to escape the opportunity since the boy was already so docile and compliant to him. "Tell me about her."

Daniel stopped chewing, his cheeks swollen with bread. "Who?"

"Rowan."

For a moment, the boy chewed his bread very slowly, looking at him as if he had now grown a third head as well. "Rowan? My Rowan?"

A nerve jumped on his temple. "She's not *your* Rowan."

"I meant, my friend Rowan." He washed down his mouthful of food with some water and sighed. "There isn't much to know."

"Impossible."

"Oh, the opposite. She has no favourite colour, no hobbies and such. If she were a book, she'd be a notepad. Blank and empty."

Maybe because no one had ever even dared fill her pages. "I don't care about her hobbies, Daniel. Tell me about *her*."

He cleared his throat, looking down at the table, his brows pulling together as he tried to recall. "She's an orphan. Mmm, a soldier for some time now, and the queen awarded her the title she has a few years back after she helped the army overtake a walled city by filling their venting system with smoke." He shook his head. "I was just a bladesmith's errand boy at the time, but I remember the songs they sang about her that day and when the queen rode to our camp to hand her gratitude. That is when I knew she had to be the one to train me. A few days after that I became her apprentice. After some relentless begging." Daniel hummed, trying to think harder. "She also took quite an interest in mathematics when we took over a scholar city a few years back. She says everything has an angle if you look at it in the right way. Never understood what she meant, I failed mathematics as a boy." He turned to Elijah, a worried look crossing his stare. "What is it that you are looking to find out?"

"Nothing in particular. Wipe that strange look off your face. You can't protect her from me even if the Gods had given you that power."

Daniel's features shifted, and he suddenly no longer looked like a boy. "You wish to harm her?"

"On the contrary. I want her to harm me."

His confused brows shot up. "Eh?"

Elijah stood, patting his shoulder. "More mathematics, Daniel. Do not worry yourself with it."

She was waiting for him when he left the dining area. "Stay away from him."

"I have very little interest in your friend, Rowan."

"Then don't speak to him."

A sharp shard of jealousy pierced him right in his chest. "He spoke to me. It would have been rude to not speak back."

Her eyes narrowed on him before she turned on her heels and left.

He would have followed after her, but she looked like she needed the time alone. Especially after he'd seen the look on her face earlier that day after she'd given the three soldiers their poisoned food. The way her gaze had drowned in utter desolation was something that would haunt Elijah forever.

Sleep found it hard to possess her despite the exhaustion in her bones after a whole day of training and attempting to evade being found by the pesky God of War. Sleep was finding it even harder to approach her especially when a certain frog had taken to singing its sonnets right outside her tent.

Throwing her blanket off, Rowan groaned.

The damn frog. Wouldn't. Shut. Up.

Grabbing her sword, she slid her cold feet through her boots, not even bothering to tie them, and stomped outside.

Where was it?

She chased the sound and then crouched by a bush, squinting, and trying to catch a look inside of it.

"What are you doing?" a smooth, cold voice whispered right in her ear.

Rowan jerked back, falling on the muddy ground when she raised her sword at him. Surrendered, she dropped her entire body to the ground, throwing her arms wide and sighing as she sank in the dirt.

At least the stupid frog had stopped croaking.

She could fall asleep right there as she was.

That one second of relaxation came to a very abrupt halt when she realised what she was wearing. A long man's shirt about five sizes too big and cotton trousers that were one step closer to turning transparent on the next wash.

Rowan sat up, so fast that the God of War took a step back to avoid being tackled. "Have you no manners, you absolute psychopath?"

"Psychopath?" He blinked. "I'm not the one going after a small amphibian carrying a sword. At least give the poor frog a fighting chance."

Just then, the frog croaked again, almost as if to validate his words, bringing Rowan one step closer to insanity. "Shut up!" she screamed at it, feeling the lack of sleep make her sway on her feet.

"You need sleep."

She pointed her heavy sword at him. "What I need is for you to disappear. Forever."

He tipped his chin in the sword's direction. "Then use it."

"I'm trying to give this poor God a fighting chance."

War's mouth twitched, pulling into a smirk. "Head back to sleep, I'll deal with the frog."

Rowan fashioned one massive curtsey. "Oh, but what a thoughtful God you are, your clement holiness."

Running a dirty sleeve over her nose, she glowered at him and backed away to her tent. But a faint whisper caught her ear, and she stopped, holding in her breath so she could take in more of the words. Once she grabbed a sense of where they were coming from, she quietly dragged her tired self there, hiding behind a tree that faced Adam's and Henry's tent.

A queen's guard had arrived at the camp, already talking to Adam, and no one had called for Rowan. Something she found unsavoury as a fellow compeer.

That unsavouriness turned to suspiciousness when a few sleepy captains made their way to the tent, led by Henry. Daniel among them.

What had he done now?

"You all swore an oath to your queen," Adam said to them, and they all straightened their spines at that. "You will swear another one here today. Whatever order of hers will be passed to you today mustn't pass to anyone else beside the one you see next to you. Are we clear?"

"Clear," they all repeated, no longer groggy, and ready to obey.

When she made her way back to camp, she found War sitting on a rock, juggling a couple of pebbles in his hands. "Did you quit being holy to juggle for a living? We've needed a jester around here to lift spirits."

"She's full of jokes tonight," he said, smiling up at her, not the least bit offended. He never had looked offended. Rowan thought she might need to try harder.

"Don't you sleep?"

"Not really."

She was envious.

"Give it up, Rowan," he said. "Walk to the infirmary and get something to help you sleep."

"They make you slow."

"This clement holiness will kick coal over you if something

happens."

She caught herself before she could smile. "Who will kick coal over me when you do something?"

"Like what? What can I do while you're sleeping that I can't do when you're awake or when you've been asleep every other night?"

He had a point. She still didn't trust him though. Who in this shitty realm could ever trust him? But she thought about it for a moment, and there was no choice left for her but what he'd said.

"Though," he called as she made to head for the infirmary. "You could use a bath before sleep."

Her eyes drew shut. Partially from embarrassment and partially because the thought of washing up almost made her cry when she was this desperate for sleep. For a brief second, she considered sleeping with dried mud and gods knew what else was all over her, but she had yet to lose that much of her dignity. She didn't even consider lighting a fire to heat up the water. A cold wash it was.

"Whose shirt was that?" War called from outside her tent as she began undressing.

Why did he want to know? Bored? Trying to annoy me? "Some dead soldier's. A tall one."

"Did you not know his name?"

"Why would I?"

"You said he was tall. *Tall* must have had a name."

"I knew he was tall because of the stupid size," she almost shouted. "We pick sleeping clothes from piles dropped after battles belonging to the fallen soldiers."

"I see."

She paused her scrubbing, frowning at herself. There had been humour in his voice. She pulled her tent curtain back a little to scowl at him, only to find him smiling at himself. "All jolly topics for you, I suppose."

He looked up at her, his smile turning into a grin. "Don't forget your face, little thief," he said, tapping a finger on his cheek.

Rowan let the curtain fall and hid back inside her tent, scrubbing at her face a little more roughly than normal. When she'd gotten all of her skin and hair clean, and her teeth had begun chattering, she left her tent for the infirmary.

Of course, he followed after her like a lost puppy.

"It's the other way around, Rowan," he murmured in her ear.

She paused, glanced around, and then turned towards the other side of the camp when she realised he had been right.

He put a hand on the side of her arm when she swayed on her feet, and she jerked back as if his touch had been burning coals instead. "Don't ever do that again."

"Help you?"

"Touch me."

"It was barely that, Rowan."

"It's enough you breathe around me."

"It really is."

She glanced up at him and frowned. Why the hell did he make so little sense all the damn time?

"You're going to trip if you keep looking at me."

Rowan looked away, angry at herself for even being curious enough to give a shit about him. "Why do you care?" she spat, pulling back the infirmary tent curtain and stepping inside.

The night nurse dozing off on her chair jerked up from her seat. Her eyes wide more on Rowan than on the God of War. "R-Rowan?" the old woman stammered as if she was seeing a ghost.

"I need something to help me sleep."

"To sleep?" The confused nurse quickly rushed to her cabinets, stumbling on her feet a couple times. Pulling back a sachet, she handed it to Rowan. "Noreberry powder. You can use them fresh as well if you find them in the forest."

Rowan shook her head. "They resemble haleberries too much." One of the most poisonous little things in this realm. Death's fruit.

"Ah," the nurse said, her eye twitching a little as a droplet of sweat fell down her temple. "They do, you're right." She turned her feigned laughter and smile to War. "She's right. Good thing she is so smart."

"Good thing," War agreed, smiling back at her. Giving the nurse a polite nod, he followed after Rowan again and into the night as she veered around the tents.

"Why did you pick them the other night?" he asked.

"Picked up what?"

"The haleberries. If you knew what they were, why did you pick them?"

That made her still. "Maybe I have a taste for them."

"An odd palette you have, little thief. Poison has a very acquired taste."

"Leave me alone."

"Who are you going to poison, Rowan?"

She spun to him as she reached her tent. "You."

He grinned ear to ear. "Hard to believe that when you made me promise not to touch them that night. But let's say that is the truth, how were you ever going to convince me to eat them?"

"You don't need to eat haleberries. If you grind them to a very fine powder and let it touch skin, you can be rid of anyone you wish to be rid of. Let them breathe the dust and you'll be rid of them even faster."

"Terrifying." His eyes dropped to her hands laying limply on her side. And then his mouth tilted into a smirk. Probably when he noticed her pinkish fingertips from crushing the haleberries all of the afternoon. "You're truly terrifying, Rowan of Ingburn."

Rowan had never been told that. She'd heard it from others, usually whispered under their breaths. But no one had dared tell her.

"You're more terrifying to me," she admitted, wanting to feel human because being told she was something of fear made her feel entirely inhuman. It often made her think so. So often that she'd almost believed it, too.

"I stand before you unarmed, without armour, yours to kill."

"As am I."

He shook his head. "You're not mine to kill, Rowan. Even the Gods would not be that cruel to you. To make you mine to kill."

A deep ache began pulsing under her chest. "And they've made you for me to kill?"

"*I* have. I've given you that permission. You and no one else but you. Have it. Have my death."

She scoffed and stepped forward, standing almost head-to-head with him as she glared up at him. "I've yet to see through your games. But maybe they're just games of a silly bored God who had nothing better to do but meddle in human affairs."

"Maybe." He reached a hand forward to push a single coiled hair strand that had fallen over her eyes. "Will you play along?"

Resisting the urge to lean in or away from his touch, she said, "I'm not interested."

"What a shame. I would have made it good for you." His eyes dropped to her lips, and she blinked away, looking at the dark distance of the forest instead.

He tilted his head, trying to catch her strayed gaze. "When you're not glaring, brooding, covered in mud and smoke, you're not so bad to look at."

Her mouth twitched, but she didn't let herself sneer at him, otherwise he might have thought she'd truly been offended. "Oh, but thank you, your holy divinity," she so politely crooned. And then snapped at him, "Now fuck off."

"So terribly mean," he said, not looking hurt or offended even a bit. "And so, so terribly violent." Backing away, he added, "Go sleep now, Rowan, before you strangle me."

"That doesn't sound so bad."

"I might like it."

She shook her head. "You're tiring."

"Good. Head to sleep now."

"Don't tell me what to do."

"Then stay."

She heard him chuckle when she spun and headed inside her tent. The noreberry powder dissolved in her water cup, sitting at the bottom, and she stared at it for a long while—so long that sleep began calling for her without its help. Shooting a look at the tent's entrance, she set the cup on a stool and laid down on her mattress. A sense of safety settled in without her even realising. That same sense of safety drew more sleep in until her lids felt heavy, and she was jumping inside nightmares.

Six poppies

SOMETHING HAD BOTHERED ROWAN since the night when she'd seen Adam and Henry lead a few captains inside the generals' tent. It had bothered her even more when she'd waited for days to no end for Daniel to confess to her that he'd been called by Henry and Adam, and what for.

So, she'd lied and sent word to the front guard to head for lunch as someone else would take on his shift soon, and then she'd waited until Adam and Henry pulled most soldiers to train by the river back because of the humidity, far enough for her to search their tent without being caught—a place Rowan wasn't really allowed to be in despite her status. She had her own general's tent. On the other side of the camp. Adam and Henry trusted her to win their queen's war, but not enough to hear her direct orders or reports. It had been so long since she'd directly heard back from Mugril that she had started wondering if the city she'd been born in even existed anymore.

A shiver went down her spine when her senses warned her

about another presence inside the tent. She was being watched. As she had been watched for the past two weeks. "What are you doing here?" she asked, continuing to carefully rummage through the letter stacks, hoping to find the latest order sent by their queen.

His tall shadow fell over her when he leaned in to take a closer look at what she was doing. "Could ask you the same. When I saw you lure that poor soldier away, I knew you were up to no good."

"Did anyone see you?"

"I'm hard to miss."

She groaned, turning to him. "You want to get me killed?"

He looked down at her. "No, but it looks like you want to get yourself killed."

"No one saw me."

"I saw you."

"Will you tell?"

"Tell what?"

She rolled her eyes. "You're annoying me."

"Already catching feelings for me, Rowan?"

"Annoyance is hardly something you want me to catch."

He leaned against Adam's table and threw one of his lemon sherbets in his mouth. "I can go slow."

"As can I," she mindlessly said, searching through the many letters. "When I drive a knife through your gut and hear you painfully moan every note on the musical alphabet."

"Now that was poetic and rather romantic."

Slowly, she rolled her eyes up at him to glare. "You know what my favourite thing is? Some like to sneak up on prey. I like to befriend it and make it believe I am harmless."

"You've not befriended me or showed me in any way that you're harmless."

"You seek my company, and you feel comfortable enough to be unarmed around me."

He blinked to himself, crushing the lemon sherbet between

his teeth. "You make a good point."

"Don't crush the candy. It's obscene."

"I'm impatient." He lifted a piece of paper up from Adam's desk. "Are you looking for this?"

Rowan almost ran to him and reached to grab the letter, only for him to quickly pull it out of her reach and over his head. He had to be at least six feet and seven or eight inches because his stretched arm touched and bent at the top of the eight-foot tent.

"Give it to me," she hissed.

"If only there was a nice word used to persuade people to do kind gestures for others."

Groaning, she rested a knee on the table and climbed it. She did it so fast and unexpectedly that he just stood there gaping when she plucked the letter from his fingers.

Still reeling from the shock, he remained as still as a statue as Rowan quickly unfolded the letter holding the latest orders from the queen.

Her quick breaths halted, seized altogether at the words written on it—the orders their queen had given. "She wants to send a battalion to raid the nearby Gobresh villages before their infantry reaches us for the last battle. She wants us to *take* the babies and the small Gobresh children." Folding the paper, she put it back on the table and braced her hands against it, willing her mind to stop spinning so fast.

Even the God of War didn't seem amused anymore.

Heavy footsteps marched towards the tent, angry voices accompanying them.

Rowan's heart started racing, and so did her movement. She pushed hard at Elijah's chest until his back met the tall cupboard Adam and Henry used to store their armours. "Get in."

He blinked confused. "In where?"

"In there."

Elijah's eyes widened just a fraction. "Why?"

"Because they will see us."

"Why wouldn't I want them to see us?"

"We can't be here," she hissed, looking back at the entrance where Henry and Adam had stopped to chastise the soldier for leaving his post.

War tilted his head to her. "No, *you* can't be here."

She groaned, pulling the cupboard doors open and shoving him inside the tiny space before squeezing herself in there, too. Rowan thanked every God there was that the cupboard was empty and big enough for the elephant of a man War was.

The space around them fell in total darkness when she pulled the cupboard doors shut, closing them in. The only small flash of light came through the tiny crack between the doors where Rowan could see the two generals usher inside the tent along with a few others.

His and her breaths were so in sync that Rowan had not noticed yet how close they were to one another. When she did, she held in her breath just to feel his.

"Breathe, Rowan," he murmured in her ear.

And so she did, her chest rising until it felt like it could burst.

Elijah chuckled, and she shifted to spin around and put a hand over his mouth. "Shut up."

His brows hiked up, and she felt him smile against her palm.

"East," Rowan heard Adam's faint voice say. "We enter east first. Their villages have had the least damage from this war and they've had plenty of crops so their kind is the healthiest and probably the least diseased."

"Rowan would know an entire battalion has disappeared from camps, she counts almost every single soldier every morning and evening," Daniel chimed in, and she could tell from the way his sentence faded that the two other generals had given her captain a silencing look.

Henry sighed. "Rowan will not be part of this."

"Because she'd be against it," Daniel continued, and that somehow made Rowan let herself proudly smile just the slightest. "We were ordered to not harm civilians and that our march over Gobresh would be solely to claim lands."

"It was an order!" Adam bellowed, banging his fist on the table.

Rowan flinched, and both of Elijah's arms went around her, engulfing her in an embrace and holding her shaking body in his. Some small part of hers wanted to lean into him, to hide in his hold, to smother herself against his scent of sandalwood.

Ignoring the conversation outside, she looked back up at him. Realisation struck her a little too sharply and she pulled back the best she could inside the small space, his embrace coming loose, too. "Don't touch me."

"There is nowhere for me to go, little thief."

She shot him a cold look that did none of what it was supposed to do.

War hummed. "Strange."

"What is?"

"Your perfume," he murmured. "You smell delicious."

Rowan swallowed. "It's just rosemary. I was always told it keeps the flies away." She looked up at him. "But apparently it doesn't work for all kinds of flies."

Dropping his head back, he bit his lip and chuckled softly, his shoulders silently shaking. "Hard to breathe again, Rowan?"

It was. Everything was too warm under her thin clothing that was accordingly appropriate for the southern climate. Rowan always made sure to feel the least uncomfortable she could. Sweat and frost made her thinking slow, sluggish, and sometimes it made it unbearable for her to be inside her own head, her own skin. But despite all the effort she'd spent in buying the freshest linen fabric to make heat less bothersome, it wasn't working. She felt terribly warm.

She turned her back to him again, closing her eyes and hoping he wouldn't hear her quiet plea, "Please stop."

And he did.

Something that surprised her because he'd never done as she'd asked or ordered—in fact, he'd always done the opposite. "You stopped," she whispered, frowning to herself. "I don't remember hitting you in the head."

"You said please."

She found herself turning to look at him over her shoulder.

"What?" he asked, gently tapping his finger on her nose.

Her eyes almost twisted to look down at where he'd just touched her. Shocked to say the least, her mouth opened and closed a few times, unable to find any words. "I'm trying to figure out what exactly makes you such a moronic God."

"You'll have to keep looking long and hard for an answer to that, little thief. Good thing I don't mind."

"You're an idiot."

"If you were any nicer to me, I'd honestly turn pretentious. It would all go to my head."

"At least something would," she muttered between her teeth, turning her attention to the conversation between the generals and her treacherous pupil who'd joined the conspiracy against her.

"I wouldn't be angry with him," he said close to her ear, and she felt a shiver snake down her spine and around her stomach, pooling right between her thighs. And she'd never hated her traitorous body more than at that moment. The worst part was that he had no clue of what he'd done to her, and went on, "They probably involved him knowing he'd come to you if he saw something strange. By forcing him into being their ally, he can't, otherwise he'd be a traitor."

"He should've become a traitor," she said, feeling something wrap around her throat and squeeze. "Better a traitor—"

"Than what you will do to him for being their ally?" he finished for her.

"Yes," she breathed.

"Why are you determined to aid your enemy?" Elijah asked. "Lying about the river tide, sneakily reading things that weren't meant for your eyes, lying to your queen, lying to your friend, saving the Gobresh girl from your soldiers, and so many more things that would bring you death."

Her eyes were on Daniel, the boy she'd raised herself. "I am not aiding the enemy."

"Then let them do this. This is it. The end of this war."

"But is it?" she asked. "If they take the children, it means they've been asked to kill everyone else. And one day, those babies and those children will grow to be men and women. Angry men and women who will want their revenge. One war will end a few days from now, and another one will start a few years from now. This isn't the last one. You can't say it is the last one, can you?"

He was quiet for a moment. "No. Maybe not anymore."

"See? What will be different in the next war is that the Gobresh younglings will grow along the Mugril. Make them sisters, brothers, wives, husbands, friends, and family. They will make one another kin. Then they will slay one another yet again."

"So little faith you have."

"I have no faith at all," she whispered. "There is no such thing as peace. Only fragile concord. You can't force unity between the slaughterer and the slaughtered. One will always want to hold the axe."

"You'd rather your people murder them all?"

"No, I'd rather they do not. But between this and that, maybe their death is the least cruel thing to do."

It's the least cruel thing to do. That is what she'd always told herself when she'd done what she did best—be cruel. That is what she'd told herself when she'd done everything to avoid battles, when she'd convinced Henry and Adam to not lead their honed soldiers to slaughter Gobresh soldiers who were as young as thirteen and as old as seventy because their armies had not been enough to battle the Mugril. No one had caught her yet. No one had caught her cheating battles. They'd celebrated her instead. For being cruel. As if war wasn't the cruellest thing there was. She'd seen it. It wasn't. At night, when she closed her eyes, all she could see was young boys dressed as men, wailing for their mothers as they bled into the soil of their home.

"Tell her," Daniel insisted, and Rowan's eyes fell on her friend again. "At least let's tell her. Even if she says no—"

"That girl is a monster and we both know it," Adam sneered, and Rowan felt her entire body go rigid at his words. "If she were to find out we are doing something she won't like, it is not beyond her to make us dig our own grave before she somehow makes us bury ourselves in them, too."

"If you're so afraid of her, why keep her as a general? Why give her so much power?" another captain asked, one whose name Rowan couldn't particularly recall.

"The queen likes her, and we would have never made it far enough in this war without someone who thinks like a monster. We can main and slay, but we can never have the guts to do what she does. Her mind is another form of twisted that none of the men in our ranks possess."

Her eyes pricked with the sting of tears. Not because she was upset at how they were talking about her. But because they were right. The least cruellest thing to do was still cruel. She didn't know who she had sold her soul to in exchange for the numbness in her heart, but she knew who had paid the price for it.

Her whole chest shook from her quiet laughter as she lowered her face on her palms to muffle the pouring amusement that threatened to tear through her chest and eat all of them alive.

"We are all monsters of another's creation, aren't we?" War's cold, velvety voice spoke, but not from behind her.

She lowered her hands from her face and turned to him, only to find herself alone in the cupboard. Quickly, almost giving herself away, she looked through the cupboard door crack, searching for him.

The God of War had leaned against Adam's table, picking up another of his lemon sherbets, while the rest of the room had gone quiet at his near presence.

"Aren't we?" he repeated, a little louder and more annoyed.

"I suppose we are," Henry answered, sending a cautious look to Adam.

"Who does she call her creator?" War asked, crossing his thick arms over his broad chest. "You?"

She didn't think Henry even realised that his gaze strayed to Adam after War's question.

Almost offended, the silver haired general sneered at his old friend. "What are you insinuating, Henry? That I made her evil?"

Henry's grey scowl deepened. "No one said that."

The tension in the small tent turned blistering hot and cold at the same time. Accusing and angry looks were thrown around at each other. Simple words were said, all misinterpreted by the other, exaggerated by the other. Rowan could easily understand that none of them had any meaning behind. She knew men like Adam and Henry would not care for War's words. So it all took her by surprise.

The commotion was terrifying.

It rose as fast and burst as fast as a volcano.

Friends accused one another, threatened one another.

Weapons were raised.

Promises of blood were made.

"Stop," Rowan murmured to herself. "Please stop."

War raised his eyes to where she hid, and smirked.

Like someone had clicked their fingers and ordered a halt, the commotion ended.

Confused, Henry and Adam looked at one another, staggering out of the tent, wondering and confused about what they had just done.

Rowan had just seen War's power.

She'd seen what he could do.

"Come out now," he told her, picking up Adam's whole container of lemon sherbets.

Her back slid against the cupboard, and she dropped to the ground, taking in the darkness around her and the little sliver of light framing him.

The small space hugged its suffocating walls around her, and for the first time in a while, she let herself pretend she was being consoled in someone's embrace. The darkness had been the only thing that had really ever held her. Wrapping her arms around herself, she held tightly.

A silent sob shook her chest.

Then another.

Her body trembled from her quiet cries. Tears rolled down her face. She dropped her head back, her eyes falling to his again, finding him utterly still. She was sure he couldn't see her or hear her, but she might have been wrong.

He didn't move until her throat grew hoarse and her body went slack from the taunt cries she'd suppressed. Defeated by her own emotions, she laid there until she was drained.

All while he stood on the other side of the darkness. Watching her.

Rowan had never cried in front of anyone. Never had shed a tear when she'd been hurt or bleeding. Even over her parent's grave, she had not shed a single tear. She couldn't. She didn't know her parents well enough to miss them, to need them, to seek them at night when she'd had nightmares. Rowan had never cried before because of her rotten fate that had brought her this far and shaped her to be the monster Adam had talked about.

But she did because of him.

She didn't want to be defended, justified. Not by him out of all. But out of all…he'd been the only one to ever do so. Without a single doubt. As if he had not witnessed her monstrous ways.

Maybe it was just one monster defending another monster.

But at that moment, it had not mattered.

Rowan had thought about it long and very hard before she'd stomped to where he had sat just outside of their camp, sunbathing on top of a flat rock slightly raised from the ground, and eating more lemon sherbets.

"Delay them," she plainly said.

He smiled up at the blue skies, or perhaps at her. "Even in my dreams you sound angry."

She kicked his foot, and the ancient God jerked upright, shocked at her gesture more than angry. "Did you just...kick me?"

"Delay. Them."

He scowled and stood. "Who?"

"Adam's battalion heading towards Gobresh."

"I can't interfere in this, Rowan."

She swallowed hard, phantom claws trapping her next words in her throat, trying to pull them back down to the pits of her pitiful insides that had surrendered to hopelessness. "Please," she uttered the words in one shaky breath.

Those violent eyes of his hardened. "Rowan–"

She fell down to her knees before him, and begged, "Please."

The look on his face was nothing short of terrifying, stern shadows falling over his features. "Why do you want to prevent this war that hasn't even happened yet?"

Rowan shook her head, and begged again, "Please, just grant me this." Her eyes lowered. "I-I will be her. I will be whoever you wish me to be. I'll pretend."

"Get up, Rowan."

She didn't.

"Rowan, get up," he called with none of his usual humour or amusement.

Looking up, she found him standing over her, his hand stretched to her. "Will you do it?"

"I will. Now, get up."

Wincing, she put a palm to her aching knee. "My knee is locked. Give me a minute," she said truthfully. She had very bad joints. It was what heavy training and many days sleeping against cold surfaces did to one's body.

He hooked his arms under her shoulders and hoisted her up like she was a toddler, all one hundred and forty pounds of her. Once she was on her feet, he bent down on one knee and shook the dirt from her legs.

Rowan almost recoiled at that, looking around the camp to make sure no one could see the God of War kneeling before her and cleaning her up.

He got up, raked one last look over at Rowan, and then turned towards the forest.

"Where are you going?" she asked.

"To delay them."

Impatiently, she chewed on the stolen lemon sherbets War had left behind as she waited for his return.

Would he really delay them?

Could he?

Why would he do that in the first place? Maybe he had just lied to her. Deceived her. Or he would do neither of those since he'd told her that he had no desire in such things. And she'd believed him then. But maybe he had changed his tune now.

The air shifted, suddenly blowing north.

"You ate them all?"

She coughed at his sudden appearance, almost choking on the candy.

He patted her back, and she jumped to her feet, trying to get away from him.

War raised both of his hands up, his eyes lowering, but Rowan had caught the glimpse of hurt that had flashed against the violet. "Apologies. I didn't mean to scare you."

He didn't scare her. Not like he'd thought, at least. "You're back."

"I am," he said, laying down on his rock again. "The soldiers are also returning. Slower, but they are."

"They are?" she asked, astound. How had he done it?

"Is that doubt in your voice, Rowan?"

"It is."

He smiled. "No need for it. I am the God of War, King of the Gods."

"I know. But what I don't know is your intention. Why would you help me?"

"You asked."

It simply couldn't have been that *simple*. "I'm sure many have asked you to do things for them since you have joined this camp."

"And maybe I have obliged."

"Have you?"

"No," he said, pensively. "No, Rowan, I haven't."

"You helped me because I look like her, didn't you?"

The pensiveness in his eyes and voice grew dour. "Yes."

"That was a lie, wasn't it?" Though it had been only a few days, she could easily tell his lies, mostly because she hadn't heard any from him thus far. Something which struck her as odd considering that it took Rowan much longer to distinguish human lies. Humans were good liars—terrific even. They lied to the point of self-destruction. They lied until they believed their own lies, until they manifested them into reality. They lied until they had manipulated their own minds, until the lie had grown into an ugly disease which they couldn't get rid of. Rowan knew. Rowan had been living with that disease herself. It was killing her. Maybe it would kill her. Some nights she hoped it would. Though...some nights she prayed it didn't, that the Gods would also choose the least cruel thing to do with her life. That they'd allow her death to be swift.

"It was," he admitted.

She forced her feet forward until she was standing near his rock, compelled by his lie and her desire to dissect it. Carefully, she sat down beside him. "Why do you sit here?"

"I've got a great view."

Rowan tilted up her head to look at the skies only to find them as arid, as blue, and as insipid as they had always been. "Your world must be so different from this one. No one would consider this a great view," she said, looking back down at him, finding him already looking back at her. It flustered her even though she had tried to not let herself be flustered by him.

"On the contrary. It's spectacular."

Rowan swallowed hard, and even though she wanted to look away from him, she couldn't. Instead, she found herself compelled to ask, "What was her name?"

His eyes almost swallowed her entirely, roaming over every inch of her face, watching certain features more intently than others. "She had many names. Thousands of them. A new one in every life she lived."

"What do you call her?"

"Mine."

Rowan felt a shiver down her spine and a twinge of that sour and unpleasant taste of envy hit the bottom of her stomach. "You don't call her by any name?"

"Only when I miss her, Rowan. I do not invoke her name unless."

Her chest felt so heavy, her breaths restricted. And she didn't know why. "How do you know she is dead?"

He stared at her for a while before answering, "I saw her eyes."

Empathy had bid her goodbye a long while back, but her heart sank a little at his words, at the thick sadness behind his deep voice. "Maybe she was playing you a trick. You should have felt for a pulse," she attempted to joke, but it fell entirely flat.

"I don't think it was wise for me to touch her."

Rowan winced. She'd heard of the disease south of Mugril, the one that had eaten through animal and human alike until they had burned villages with all of its occupants to get rid of it. Maybe she had been one of them. Could he have caught the disease, too? Strange.

"Why are you curious about her?" he asked, and Rowan froze at the question.

"You sound almost human when you talk about her," she said truthfully, only to then lie, "There are many ways to kill a human heart. And I know them all."

"You don't have to plot my death, little thief," he said, smiling up at the skies. "If you would ask me to guide your blade directly to my heart, I gladly would."

"Why?"

His smile grew bigger. "I am an unreasonable God."

"You are. But that is also a lie."

He chuckled. "Because it would mean something. My blood in your hands would mean something."

"To who?"

"To me."

"I still don't understand a thing," she said, sighing and taking a lemon sherbet. "How did you delay them?"

"I can't tell you."

"Why not?"

"It wasn't the least cruel way to do it. I could have been...nicer."

She stared at her stained hands. "You think that would have disappointed me somehow?"

"Yes."

"Why does it even matter?"

"Can't tell you," he said, taking a lemon sherbet and crushing it between his teeth.

She sighed. "Stop crushing the candy."

"Told you. I am impatient. Long games are not for me. I get straight to the point. Aim directly at what I want, not around it."

"So much philosophy behind a candy."

"I apply my philosophies on much finer things, too, Rowan." He flashed her a slow smile. "If the finer things would let me, of course."

Seven poppies

THE EVENING'S MOONLIGHT WAS as elegant as moonlight could ever be. But it became even more impeccable when it fell over her body. Sunken in the middle of the pond she'd found near the camp, Rowan had tipped her head back, letting the silver shine cast shadows all over her face.

"You will shrivel like a prune if you stay in there any longer," he said.

She didn't look surprised hearing his voice, probably having heard him approach or maybe expected him to be there. "And you will bleed red like a beetroot if you do not stay where you are."

"Maybe I don't bleed red. Maybe I bleed black," Elijah said, approaching the edge of the pond and sitting down. "Come out, and I will let you find out."

She sank further down, only her eyes visible above the water surface. Eyes that were making Elijah rethink the offer. And perhaps make another one.

"I won't look," he said, trying his best not to seem too happy about the situation they were in.

That made her rise up again, not to come out, but to say, "Because I will pluck your eyes out."

"What a horrible thing to say to someone," he said, feigning upset.

Eyes mad and mouth pulled into a snarl, she jumped, almost coming out of the water entirely. But to Elijah's unfortunate luck, she realised the state of her nakedness too soon, covering her chest with both arms. "Leave."

Without intention, his expression fell, and so did his gaze. No longer on her face. No longer on the strength she carried in her expression. But on the scars littering her skin from the neck down. Her arms. Her stomach. Her shoulders.

She ducked down in the water again, breathing hard. "Pass me my towel."

Somehow, he'd managed to get up and grab her towel, and then stepped in the pond, fully clothed. Once he was near enough, he opened the towel for her. And for some reason, she quietly turned round and let him wrap it over her shoulders. Just not before he had gotten to face the rest of her scars on her back.

He'd seen many scars on many bodies in many lifetimes.

They'd never bothered him. He had many of his own, too.

But her scars weren't just scars. They became his wounds.

Elijah sat at the edge of the pond, staring at the silvery waters quiet down as Rowan left them to get dressed. "You should let someone stitch the wound on your shoulder."

There was a pause in her movement. "It will heal just fine as long as I keep it clean."

"Rowan," he called her name like a prayer made to a cruel God who would not listen—and the cruel God she was would never listen to someone like him.

Rowan's back was still to him. Her shoulders started to rise faster, more uncontrollably, so unlike her usual, quiet self. He could hear her rapid breaths even from where he stood. "Quit thinking I'm her," was all she said, picking up the rest of her clothes and heading back to the camp.

But he wasn't thinking she was *her*.

He wasn't thinking at all.

He had not followed after her, but he'd stood before her tent's entrance for the past hour and a half. Expecting to smell the scent of disinfectant or hear her struggle while sowing her wound up.

But there was none of it.

And tired of waiting, he stepped inside her tidy, small space made up of a foldable mattress, table, chair, small stool, two buckets, and a bag.

She sat up from the bed, scooting away from him and reaching for a dagger hidden under her pillow.

Unbothered by her threats, he reached her table and dug through her small pile of possessions until he managed to find a box with a needle, thread, gauze, and some disinfectant that all soldiers were usually given. Something struck him. None if it looked used. All was still in its sterile packaging.

"I'll do it myself," she said, lifting her palm to him.

"You can't or you would have already done so."

"I can," she answered quickly, breathing fast. "I swear I can. Just give it to me." When he didn't move or give in to her request, a look of desperation crossed her lifeless face. "Please." She let out a trembling sigh, and repeated, "Please."

Elijah couldn't understand her pleas or the desperation be-hind them, but he put the sewing box at the edge of her bed, ever so slowly because she was shaking and looking like a scared little animal that was about to run away if he made any sudden movement.

Backing away from her just as slowly, he took a seat on the

stool at the far edge of her small tent and remained there, watching—helplessly watching. That had always been his true curse. To helplessly watch.

Rowan reached for the box with a trembling hand and pulled her loose shirt down her shoulder, revealing the wound that was now an angry red. Glancing at him from time to time, she began dabbing a cotton of alcohol around it, wincing and muffling a small, tearless sob every once in a while. A whimper escaped her when she made that first stitch. He didn't know why. The wound had to hurt more left as it was. It must have hurt the same ever since she'd gotten it. Elijah couldn't understand why she—the great bearer of pain that she was—couldn't endure the sting of a needle on skin that should have already been numb from burning pain and infection.

Feeling the wound around with her shaky fingers, she tried to push the needle through it a second time and failed. It was too far out of her reach and sight. After struggling with it for what seemed like too many hours, she raised two surrendered green eyes up at him.

No words were exchanged.

Not a single one.

But Elijah stood, and just as slowly as he'd left her, he neared her again. Without being told to or asked to, he took the bloodied needle from her fingers and looked at her, seeking permission down the abyss of her soulless eyes. Hoping he might find her soul down there too now that she'd surrendered something to him.

He heard her hold in a breath when his hand rested next to the wound, touching her warmed skin.

"How do you know how to do that?" she quietly asked, her voice low and tired.

"Have watched it being done more times than one can count." But what Elijah couldn't understand was why did it feel different this time? Why he not only wanted to step in and help, but he *needed* to. "Why don't you stitch your wounds?" All of her scars had healed horribly.

"Why does it matter? If *Death* wishes to take me, he will take me." She pulled her shirt forward to show him a scar on her chest. "That was the very first one. I realised that week I spent with fever that if I didn't die then, I would never die if it wasn't meant to be." Her teeth dug on her bottom lip, attempting to stop the gentle tremble. Once she caught her rapid breaths, she sighed, and said, "I was right."

"It isn't always just about death."

"It is," Rowan said, resting her chin on top of her knees, her eyes dropping to the ground, ever so lost. "If I take care of them, I feel like I'm begging him to let me live longer, or as if I am showing him that I am trying to live longer. I don't want him to think that." Turning her face away, she ran her sleeve over her green eyes that she was now hiding from him, and whispered, "You better tell him that you forced me to do this."

Elijah had frozen at her words. The ache in his heart had never felt as raw, as red, as human as it felt at that moment. It hurt to think of how many times he'd begged *Death* to let her live since he'd found her in this realm many moons ago while she'd done everything to convince him otherwise. How many times had the King of Gods gone to his knees in front of the gates of the afterlife to beg? How many days had he spent there, waiting for *Death* to hear his pleas? So selfishly, he'd held onto the woman who reminded him of *tranquil*—of the peace he had once lost. So selfishly, he'd done it because she reminded him of his peace.

"Promise me," she said, turning her glassy eyes to him, the ones he was sure no one but him had ever seen before.

The vivid green of her irises was plagued with something else besides lifelessness. Once he saw the hopelessness there, he couldn't say anything besides, "I promise."

After stitching her wound, he stayed there a while longer, his hands still on her, breathing near her, and she let him. She even let him brush his fingers down her many scars.

Elijah frowned to himself, wondering—he'd done too much

of that lately. Why was he wondering about her scars? Why was he wanting to know? Even when he had all the answers to the questions he wanted to ask her.

She'd been made to fight. She'd been made for battle. She'd been made to bear scars.

He wondered—wondered if it had been through one of them that her soul had bled through and away from her. He wanted to find out which battle it had been, which blade, which person had held it. He wanted to hunt down that moment and see how it had happened. He wanted—he was wanting these days, too. The God of War never *wanted*. He had all he wanted. He had no desires. He fed from others' desires.

"Are you done?" she asked, her voice empty. If she had not been near enough for him to feel the vibrations of her words on his skin, he would have thought her to be far away from him. The words were so far away from her, too. So was her mind. So was her soul.

He *wanted*—he wanted to find it and give it back to her. To see how she looked with one, if she was just as exquisite with it as she was without.

"Elijah?"

"Yes, little thief?" he asked, attempting to contain the smile from his words. It was the first time she had called him by the name that the woman who had raised him had given him. There were only two creatures who were privy to that knowledge, and only those two had ever called him that. Elijah had not intended to give her his true name, but he'd also not intended to give her permission to end his life either. He felt like she owed both of those rights. To know his name and end him, too. He dared press his lips to her shoulder, smiling when she shivered and gasped. "Now I am."

"You've never told me what I've stolen," she breathlessly said, pulling her sleeve up her shoulder, her shaky fingers brushing over where his lips had just been.

"You're a very bad thief, that is why."

She shook her head. "I'm not rested enough to figure out any meaning in that."

"Is this an offer to lay with you?"

She sighed. "That's an offer for you to get the fuck out."

"Rowan, Rowan," he crooned, standing. "Stop being so horrible to me, you're going to steal my heart, too."

"You have one?"

He grinned at her as he backed away towards the exit. "Can't you hear it? It's practically screaming out your name." Placing a hand on his chest, he feigned surprise, lowering his hand to feel around, lower, and lower as if he couldn't find a heartbeat. "Wait a minute. I don't think it was my heart."

Quickly, before he could lower his hand any further down, she reached for her dagger and threw it at him. Albeit very clumsily because he easily leaned to his side, letting it pass by. But that would have made it exactly her sixth attempt on his life.

He laughed, and for a second, when she looked away from him, he thought he saw her smile.

It might have been then, or maybe even before, that Elijah realised he was falling. He didn't know exactly where or why. He'd never been a man of many questions anyway, so that mattered very little to him.

It didn't take long for him to accept it.

He was falling.

Again.

War couldn't fall.

He'd take everything with him.

"Aren't you cold out there?" she suddenly asked.

"If you're offering to cuddle with me, then yes—yes, I am very cold."

Ever so slowly, a smile curled up her lips. "I have no dagger to throw at you again."

"I'll consider you threw it anyway." Maybe she had because he was sure he was bleeding from somewhere.

She nodded, resting her chin on top of her knees as she

watched him.

There had never been such a time where his heart had felt the way it did at that moment. So heavy, so restless. "I don't think I can leave, Rowan. I don't know what to do."

"Then don't," she said, her voice small.

"Repeat it again for me. I don't think my ears believed it."

"Don't leave, Elijah. If you're mine to kill, then that would make you my hostage. Hostages can't be free."

"No, we can't be," he agreed, carefully taking a seat on the stool again. "I've always wondered what you do here alone."

She sighed and laid back down, blinking up at her fabric ceiling that fluttered and quivered at the touch of the wind and rain outside. "Waste time."

"How can time be wasted?"

"By waiting."

"Waiting for what?"

She turned her eyes to him. "The end. Not death. Just the end. The end of the day. The end of my headache. The end of this rain. The end of this war."

"An interesting hobby for certain."

Again, she smiled at him. "And you? What do you do out there?"

"I also wait."

"For what?"

Her. "You," he confessed. Elijah was not a man to shy away from making known what he wanted.

Her chest rose and fell fast with her sharp breaths, and his eyes dropped there. "A very self-destructive hobby," she calmly said even though she nervously fidgeted with a wavy strand of hair on her shoulder.

"Is that why my heart aches?"

Rowan stilled. Her eyes locked tightly on a spot on her thin tent walls. Even her chest wasn't moving anymore. She had stopped breathing entirely.

Part of Elijah liked that. Perhaps she would know just a little how he felt all the damn time. Part of him was too afraid to know her truth—that she didn't look at every sunrise like he did, hoping he'd be able to see just a glimpse of her again.

Rowan licked her lips, and hoarsely said, "I'm sure there are a thousand women out there who'd throw themselves at you without the need for you to come up with such intricate persuasions."

"Then throw yourself at me."

He'd stunned her again. "Why? Because I remind you of her?"

"Yes," he lied, the words so strange in his mouth, resonating like a pebble dropping inside an empty room.

Her lifeless gaze turned deeper, darker, endless as it bore into his. "What was her name?"

"I cannot tell you for I cannot speak her name to you."

"Why?"

"The fates want it so. It is my curse."

"*Turmoil* and *tranquil*," she mindlessly hummed. "War and—" She stood up, sitting at the edge of her bed as she looked up at him. "Peace?" She shook her head and scoffed, incredulity filling her expression. It was the most amused he'd seen her be. "It can't be this childish."

"Childish?"

"War fell in love with *Peace*?"

"I never said I was in love with her."

There was a pause. She wanted to ask him, Elijah could see it, sense it, foretold it. But the storm never came despite the turbulence.

He wouldn't have been able to tell her anything but the truth.

The truth that he was in love with her.

The truth that despite the many lifetimes he'd lived and sought her, this one had felt like the first time ever. Elijah almost felt guilty. For having loved her in this life more than any other.

But their meetings before had been short. In every lifetime he'd watch her die not long after he'd found her, they had simply not had the time to find profoundness—he'd barely had the time just to see her. In this one, she'd already been dead a long while before he came. He couldn't understand how he could love her in death. How could he fall for such a lifeless, soulless thing.

"Ask whatever you are meaning to ask," he said.

"I don't want to. I don't want to know." Those emerald soulless eyes drew darker, more haunted. "I've done heinous, vile things, but this feels the most sickening one of them all."

"What is?" he asked.

"Taking a dead woman's place."

Hope pierced him viciously. "You would want to?"

She was suddenly panting, such chaos gathered in her features that were pulled with a mix of emotions Elijah could tell apart so easily—fear, confusion, disgust, spite, hatred, desire. Only one of them was left when she rolled her eyes to him again. "I forget that you are supposed to be a horrible man, too."

"Supposed?"

She bit down on her smile. "You do a terrific job at disguising it behind this charming persona you put up."

His mouth twitched. "Charming?"

"Don't latch on my words."

"Let me, I beg." He got up and kneeled before her. When she tried to lean away, he pinched her chin between his fingers, his thumb brushing her skin back and forth. "Tell me how to charm you. If I say any more desperate things, the Gods are going to look down on me."

Her eyes drew shut, and a small, drowned cry came from her parted lips. "Don't do this, please."

"Do what, Rowan?"

Again, she said nothing but looked at him with beseech, silently pleading with him as if she didn't hold his heart in her hands.

Leaning in, he pressed his lips to her cheek, exhaling a trembling sigh as he did so. Then he repeated it again. He kissed her face all over, his heart beating almost out of his chest from fear that she would ask him to stop.

She didn't touch him back, she didn't move at all, she simply let him.

When he rested his brow on hers, he noticed the unshed tears slowly roll down her cheeks. He would have leaned and kissed them all away, but he was entirely too fascinated to move.

She reached to wipe them away, but he grasped her wrist.

"There it is," he said. "It was just hiding away."

"What is?" she whispered.

"Your pretty soul."

More tears drenched her skin.

"Why was it hiding?" he asked, brushing his thumb over her stray tears.

She shook her head. "Why are you doing this to me?"

"What am I doing to you, Rowan?" He had never wanted to know something more desperately. So desperately that he'd lay his Dawnbringer at her feet and ask her to take his life with his own blade before he'd have to wait another minute without her answer.

"I don't want to hurt."

"Is that why it was hiding away? Because you don't want to hurt?"

"Elijah—"

"Yes, my little thief, invoke me, chant my name like a curse and let me haunt back those who have haunted you."

Carefully, she reached to touch his face, her shaky hand freezing midway. The tips of her fingers had barely grazed his skin, but he let out a shuddering breath and drew his eyes shut. Tentatively, she brushed her fingertips over his jaw. And even the ghost of a touch almost ruined him. He needed her to have mercy. He needed her to spare him even though he'd given her permission to be the one to end his life.

And then she did—she leaned in and pressed her lips to his jaw. Barely a touch. Barely a kiss. "Please go," she breathed, dropping her head on his shoulder.

"Don't ask me that."

She sucked in a stuttering inhale, her whole body shaking with a silent cry. "You're not mine, Elijah. I don't want you to go, but you're not mine. You belong to someone else. I can't pretend nearly as well as you do."

In all the time that he'd lived, he'd never felt his heart break the way it had at those words, at the anguish bleeding along them. How could he tell her—how could he tell her something he couldn't speak of? How could he tell her that he belonged to her?

"Please go," she said, pulling back and away from him, hugging her knees to her chest. "Elijah, please."

"I wish I had not taught you this trick," he said, reaching to leave a kiss on her brow. "I have no choice but to obey."

"Good night," she said as he backed away to leave.

"Good night, my Rowan."

Eight poppies

THE MORNINGS AFTER THAT night had been new. She'd pretended that night had never happened, and to her luck, he'd played along. Rowan had been ready to waste her little wishes on things she couldn't afford to wish for. She'd been ready to do worse after he'd called *his* Rowan, but thankfully, he had left faster than she could react.

His shadow followed after hers as she trailed around the forest, foraging. The Gobresh lands had always been richer, more fertile. She couldn't count the number of strange consumable plants she'd come across since she'd left Mugril borders to join the infantry. Mugril was rich with mines and Gobresh was rich with produce. Mugril was much smaller in size and mostly sat between mountains and high rock while Gobresh was all fields, rivers, and rich loams, much bigger in size, too—stretching almost five times the size of Mugril. But it was the land of farmers, fisherman, forgers, builders, and mostly such pacifistic disciplines. While Mugril forged man and steel alike, with an army three times the population of the Gobresh capitol, made of men and women who had held swords before they'd held a pen. The only luck Gobresh had against Mugril in this war was its size. It had taken their infantry years to drag itself to battles across the many towns to the heart of Gobresh. Though they'd mostly won them with ease, the Gobresh had managed to wear them down enough to stretch this war longer that it should have been, and strengthened their own army with each city they'd lost.

"What is that?" Elijah asked, crouching beside her as she began picking a few green leaves.

"Basil," she said, plucking a leaf and holding it to him, expecting him to take it from her hand, not lean in and bite it from her fingers, his lips brushing over her skin.

Elijah winced. "That is pleasant to you?"

She nodded, bringing a leaf to her mouth. "Very. It's the most pleasant thing in this realm especially when you have a stomach-ache." For some reason, even after she'd answered him, he remained there. Close to her. Watching her. "What?"

"Nothing," he said, his violet eyes sinking into her face, looking so profoundly and deeply that she almost shrunk back. "And everything."

"You're a confusing man."

"I'm not a man."

She raked a look over him. "Could've fooled me."

He cocked his head back and grinned down at her. "This must be a dream. She's making more harmless jokes."

Standing, Rowan headed to another bush. "Should have just fed you poison."

"Fifteen."

"Fifteen what?" she asked.

"Fifteen times you've threatened me. Six is the number of times you've acted upon them."

She stood up and leaned against a tree. "Huh."

"Huh?" he asked, walking to her while holding a small red flower in his hand. A poppy. He tapped the flower on her nose.

"Have I counted wrong?"

Rowan had to tilt her head up to look at him with how close to her he was standing. "It seemed more in my head. Possibly because I've threatened and attempted to kill you behind your back more than fifteen times."

"That is the most romantic thing anyone has ever said to me," he said, putting the poppy behind her ear and running the back of a finger gently down her face before pulling his hand to his side.

Her mouth had gone dry, her heart had gone furious. She wasn't focused enough to think of a snarky reply or a reply at all. Besides, after that night, she didn't think they mattered anymore. He now knew she didn't mean them, so she said, "Poppies grow in graveyards. They aren't flowers you wear in your hair."

"Poppies are harmless flowers that humans have made something odious out of." He reached a hand down her braid resting over her right shoulder. "What an awful thing to do to such a beautiful flower."

For a moment, it had seemed as if he had not been talking about poppies. "Perhaps they ought to stop growing in such ominous places."

"Perhaps," he agreed, taking the end of her braid, and wrapping it around a finger. "But a flower's job is to grow. Anywhere. Its innocence is taken advantage of by men."

"His clement divinity should have been a philosopher. Besides, both of them are useless jobs."

"Believe me, if I could help what I am," he pensively said, "I still wouldn't."

She scoffed. "Arrogance is the godliest trait you've shown me so far."

His lip quirked up. "If you'd allowed me to stay last night, I would have shown you something far godlier."

Rowan gaped at him, half appalled at him for insinuating what he had and half embarrassed. Men rarely dared speak as such to her.

Chuckling, he nudged her chin up with a finger, forcing her mouth to close. "My singing abilities. I would have put you right to bed with a sonnet."

The lie had slid so smoothly from his tongue that she couldn't help but smile. "What a shame," she said, moving around the bushes and eating some more of her basil, hoping it would help stop the flutter bubbling at the pit of her stomach. "If I had known, I might have let you stay. I love a good ballad." Plucking some mint, she held it up to him. "Mint?"

Again, he ate it directly from her hand, stopping to press a light peck on her palm as well, rendering her silent and unable to think a single other thing besides his lips on her skin. "What are we looking for out here, little thief?" he asked, wincing at the taste of mint as well. "You can poison me at the comfort of your tent, too."

She looked ahead. "Looking for more noreberries. For my sleep."

He'd caught her lie far too easily, but he didn't say anything. Elijah only followed after her as she filled her pouch with the maroon-coloured berries.

When she reached the high riverbank that almost overflowed with the fastest current in the whole of Tisiania, she braced herself on a rock and leaned forward to dip her hand in it. The water was so clear. Crystal. And cold. Her reflection fluttered over its surface, her ears filled with the sound of the stream.

She felt so at peace near water. So at peace that she had not noticed the man who stood on the other side of the river bank, aiming an arrow at her.

She felt peace even as he pulled the string and let it loose.

She felt at peace even as the sharp tip came flying in her direction.

The brief hope of an end faltered when the arrow was cut in half right before her eyes by a dark sword, its hilt gleaming red from the rubies etched to it.

Elijah stood in front of her, wearing his dark armour for the first time since that day he'd arrived at their camp.

Her attention fell on the hilt again, at the rubies that suddenly melted and turned liquid, dripping over his hand and down the blade like blood.

"Leave," Elijah ordered, his voice chasing into the wind, growing louder as it echoed further and further like a tidal wave.

The Gobresh man dropped his bow and fled, running fast towards his lands.

Once he disappeared from sight entirely, Elijah turned to her.

"I thought you weren't supposed to interfere," she said, panicking.

"I am not."

She breathed hard. "What will happen now?"

"I don't particularly care," he said, his sword and armour vanishing from his body. For the first time, he looked angry. He looked angry at her, too. "You didn't move. You saw him, you probably heard him, too. You didn't move, Rowan," he said a bit louder, and Rowan flinched. His chest rose fast, his jaw was set tight. "Why do you need the haleberries you've been collecting for days now?"

As she'd thought, he'd known her lies from before. "I am fine," she said, brushing her wet hand on her shirt.

"Answer me, Rowan!"

She simply spun on her heels and headed back towards the forest. He had no right to demand anything from her.

Rowan would have kept going, but she heard a grunt and then a thud coming from behind her where she had abandoned him. She'd never run faster. Tree branches lashed at her face and body, pricking her skin until she felt the warmth of blood stick to her as she ran back to him.

He had knelt down, a bloody palm braced to the ground and another to his heart. He was breathing fast, more blood sticking to his shirt that had entirely matted to his front.

On shaky legs, she reached and knelt before him, attempting to raise his body up so she could look at his wound. "What is happening?" she breathed, pressing both of her palms against a gushing wound on his chest.

He leaned back. "What was meant to kill you is now trying to kill me."

Her eyes widened, stinging and blurring with tears. "How?"

A dark chuckle slipped out of his lips, his head tipped back and his eyes screwed shut. "Godly humour."

She rose to her feet. To get help. To find some way to stop him from bleeding. To do something. Anything. But he stopped her, his hand grabbing her wrist. "Stay."

"And watch you die?" she asked, her lip quivering.

His violet eyes opened and found hers. "It can't be that hard. Stay."

Her breaths started coming in with difficulty. Something had tightly grasped her insides and wouldn't let go. "Why are you doing this to me?"

"What, Rowan?" he asked, a smile stretching on his pain ridden face. "What am I doing to you?"

Shaking her head, she tried to leave, but his grasp on her tightened. One look back at his pleading gaze and she immediately sat back down beside him. "You're not dying, are you?" It was more of a plea than a question.

"I've told you. I can only die by your hand. You're the only one I've given permission to kill me."

She touched her fingertips to his still gushing wound. "Why isn't it healing?"

"It will. Just stay here with me," he said, reaching for her hand and lacing their bloodied fingers together. "I made a deal with *Death* and his damn evil twin."

"Evil twin?"

"*Life*, Gabriel. He loves his cruel deals, the bastard."

"What sort of deal?"

"That I would give up my immortality to them, my only condition was that I would get to choose who'd take my life."

Her blood chilled. Every other thing he'd told her came surging in at once, paralysing her limbs. "W-why? Why would you do that?"

His eyes drew shut, and he sighed. "Because I am tired. I am so tired, Rowan." He brought their laced hands to his heart. "Pity me, I beg. Pity me and take it one day. Or hate me. Do it because you hate me. Do it to get rid of me if you can't find it in your heart to pity me."

"Don't do this to me," she repeated, her heart beating madly. "You can't do this to me."

He only looked at her and then drew her to lay beside him, her head resting on his stretched arm. Their faces were close, immensely close. "Am I going to find out one day what I'm doing to you that is so unfair?" he asked, pushing her hair back from her face.

Rowan wanted to allow his touch, but she feared it would let him into her truth—that she was finding herself leaning on him. A dependency that Rowan had never allowed herself to have. One that no one had ever offered her before.

If there was one thing Rowan knew, it was that she was unwantable, unlovable.

She didn't want to make herself ever believe otherwise. She couldn't afford to think so. Especially when he thought and wished for her to be someone else.

There was an odd air that evening when they'd gathered for dinner. Rowan was still raw from what had happened that morning and the truth he'd revealed to her. She had barely noticed the soldiers from Adam's battalion that had returned from their failed mission. Their heads lowered, almost ashamed, while the rest murmured and gossiped with one another after they'd been made aware by an anonymous source about the secret mission their queen had ordered his soldiers to go on.

Elijah had still not told her how he had managed to not only delay them, but to also bring them back. He said he couldn't speak of what he had done for he wasn't meant to have done it in the first place. Then she had wondered of the consequences he would have suffered for helping her. She'd wondered if he hurt the same as anyone did. If he'd hurt for her again. If he had borne pain that was meant to be hers.

When she turned to grab a glimpse of Elijah who had sat beside her against all her pleas not to, someone else caught her attention. Her lone friend. If she could even call him that anymore.

Daniel looked ashamed, too, but he'd not lowered his head or stopped trying to get her attention all day and all evening. Rowan had a faint doubt that he'd been the anonymous source who'd told on their queen's orders. The queen who'd lost the respect of at least half the soldiers in their camp with the decision to steal the Gobresh children. For a very brief moment, Rowan wondered if there was hope in humanity. If they could change. If they would rise against the queen who'd cause so much harm on innocents. But she'd wasted her hope, too. Though they'd disagreed to what was decided, none had even breathed a syllable against it.

Two tall shadows fell before her table.

"Rowan," Henry began, throwing a look over at Adam by his side as if to seek his permission to tell her about it. "We should have come to you before planning this mission."

"You didn't," she said, shoving a spoonful of stew in her mouth. "Should've, would've, could've aren't a mage's call or spell. They won't make right what you did wrong." She pushed the rest of her plate away, already full from the bullshit.

The two generals lost half the colour on their faces, but Rowan was sure it was because she'd embarrassed them in front of Elijah. "A miscalculation," Adam simply said, throwing another knowing look over at Henry.

Rowan clicked her tongue. "No, Adam. A miscalculation can happen when I put too little poison in someone's stew or what type of stone I throw at my enemy. You simply fucked up. Have fun telling your queen that."

Elijah snorted, and every pair of eyes in the open dining hall turned to him. The famously terrifying God of War was peeling off the crust from her bread and plucking tiny pieces of the crumb to pile them on top of Rowan's soup.

She stepped hard on his foot, and his violet eyes rose to hers, looking almost hurt. "I've seen you do this before," he said, pointing to the soup bowl piled with neat pieces of bread-crumbs. "Don't you like it?"

Rowan's eye twitched, and she tried to very subtly signal her head in Adam's and Henry's direction.

Elijah's brows pulled together instead, and he pinched her chin. "What's wrong?"

"If you wanted company from our women, I could have found you a much nicer one," Adam said, throwing a sharp smile in Elijah's direction.

Except that the God of War was still looking at her, staring right down the abyss of her mind from how intently he had focused his gaze on her—she always wondered what he was searching in her stare that always had him look in there so intently, so desperately.

Elijah's head slowly turned to the two generals. His hand dropped from Rowan's face, and she awkwardly straightened. "Will you really?" War asked, stretching back on his seat, and throwing an elbow back on the chair rest.

Rowan's hardened heart cracked just a little.

"Most certainly," Henry added. "You've come down here to bless us with your witness, your presence, your holy regard. It is the least we can do."

Another crack sounded around her hollow insides when Elijah nodded.

She froze when he threw an arm around her shoulders. "I want her though."

Henry and Adam exchanged an uncomfortable smile at one another before sending a scathing look at her—one that screamed for her to obey. "Sure, of course."

Elijah shook his head. "Didn't ask you for permission." His hand moved to the back of her neck, his fingers playing with the small hair at her nape. "She needs to give it to me."

All eyes were on her now. Some almost pleading with her to give in as if the God of War would turn his rage onto them because of it.

"After she finishes her food," Elijah said, pushing the bowl before her again. "Eat, Rowan." His violet eyes rolled up to the generals, turning violent again. "Go."

Once the two generals walked their stupefied selves back to their table, he pulled his hand away from her. "Forgive me."

"For what?" she asked, blinking up at him confused.

"Touching you without permission. I don't know what came over me," he said, placing the spoon back on her hand. "Eat. It's going to grow cold."

"I'm not hungry."

"You've grown thinner since I first saw you."

"Please don't do that."

"Do what?"

"The caring part. It's making me feel guilty. I can't ever afford to feel guilt. Not with what I do. I can't feel guilty for taking a dead woman's place. I can't feel guilty for taking something meant to be hers."

"You're not taking anything. I'm giving it to you." He guided her hand holding the spoon to the soup, ladling some. "Now please eat a little." His eyes rounded with beseech. "I will tell Death I forced you. I will tell him you had no choice but to obey my order."

It was not what she worried about. Despite that, she found herself saying, "It is a deal."

Nine poppies

SUBMERGED IN WATER UP to her chin, she lifted a hand above the pond's surface and stirred the still plane, watching the small waves ripple and then disappear.

In another lifetime, she wanted to be born as a rock sitting at the bottom of a pond. Water hugging her body and never letting go.

Rowan wanted to be held.

Just once.

And she knew who she wanted to be held by.

He had been watching her again, sat just outside the shore, leaning against a tree. There was no moonlight, not much light of any sort. The creature watching her could have been a beast, a monster, it could have been anything, and she wouldn't have been able to notice.

But she knew it was him.

"Elijah," she called to him.

"Yes, my little thief?"

Rowan shivered. She didn't think it was from the cold. "Light the lantern. I can't see a thing."

He didn't answer her.

"Elijah?" she called again.

Thunder cracked the air, and she looked up at the angry dark skies right before blue lightning flashed across them. Her heart raced, and she was unable to contain the excitement from her face at the show that nature was putting before her.

A drop of rain fell on her brow. Then another. Until she stood under a shower.

Lifting both hands up to feel the rain in her palms, she spun. Her head tipped up to the skies and her eyes drew shut, a wide smile stretching on her face.

She was so envious of the rain that bitterness was going to burn a hole through her heart. If she could only be so free, so unpredictable, so unapologetic, so guiltless, so pure, and so peaceful yet so violent. Maybe she wanted to be reborn as rain. She wanted to fall with such trust and be braced by the earth below to help it grow. Rainstorms were short lived, too. A short life, but one full of meaning.

If it wasn't for the sudden chatter of her teeth, she would have remained there longer.

He was already there when she turned to him, half submerged inside water, holding a towel up to her, his figure fluttering in and out of sight because of the flashing lightning.

"Come here, Rowan."

She swam up to him and opened her arms, letting him wrap the towel around her body, hoping he couldn't see her naked through this darkness either.

Lightning flashed again and she briefly saw his eyes were on her. Even if she had not, she knew they were looking at her. She flinched a little when he touched his fingers to her shivering cheek. Rowan let him. Every time he'd touched her it had felt like a first. Tentative. Exploring. So, so innocent. Strange for a man like him.

"You're about to freeze," he said, pulling his hand back from her face and retreating away from the sound of the shifting water. "Come."

Lightning flashed again. And again, his eyes were on her. His hand stretched for her to take.

It remained extended between them for a long while before Rowan battled away every thought against taking it before she did.

The towel was entirely soaked, but thankfully he'd placed her clothes under the shade of a tall tree, and they'd remained dry. Only just briefly though, as they soaked and matted to her body as soon as she had them on. She lit her lantern and turned to him. "Will you walk back with me?" She wasn't scared, but for the first time, she didn't want to be alone.

"Did you really think I would have let you walk back alone?" he asked, removing his shirt, and throwing it over her head and helping her arms through the large sleeves.

"Aren't you going to be cold?" she asked, bringing the end of the too large sleeve to her face, inhaling the warm scent of sandalwood that clung to it from his body.

"Hold my hand and maybe I won't."

"What if I am cruel and do not care?"

"You wouldn't have asked."

"You're right."

"I am?"

"Just this once."

"I will take this small win," he said, lowering the lantern from her hand, and enshrouding their faces in darkness again. "And I will take this small secret, too."

"What secret?"

"The one only the dark has ever held. Your happiness." Elijah lowered his face close to hers, their foreheads resting against one another's. "If it only were darker longer. If it only were darker always."

"I like being near water," she confessed, offering a piece of her—of what made her happy.

"I know you do. And I am terribly envious."

"I don't mind being near you either."

His mouth twitched, and he dug his teeth on his bottom lip, barely containing his smile. "Oh?"

Rolling her eyes, she spun and headed inside the forest, feeling his warm presence right behind her, so close that she wished he'd hold her hand again.

Elijah had sat in his designated stool, watching her yet again as she dried her hair with a towel. Rowan had never known him to be so silent as he was being with her today.

When she stood in his direction, his shoulders straightened and he looked up at her, almost hopeful.

"Your hair is wet, too," she said, handing him the towel.

He took it from her hand, his gaze intent on her as she slowly backed towards her mattress and sat on it cross legged, watching him back.

"Why aren't you saying anything?" she asked after too many long minutes of silence on his behalf.

He lowered the towel from his hair. "I just want to look at you as you are now."

"You look at me all the time."

His mouth twitched. "Glad you've taken notice."

Rowan got to her feet, and he got to his feet, too, causing her to burst into giggles. "I...I was just going to take the towel from you," she said, still laughing, slowly stepping in his direction with her arms mockingly raised to signal surrender. "Just the towel. Don't be scared."

He extended the towel to her. "Can't help it."

When she grasped the other end of it, he tugged, pulling her with it. The moment their bodies touched, Rowan jumped a step back, panting. "I...I—"

"Yes?" he asked, closing the distance between them.

"Don't," Rowan murmured, flinching away from the reach of his hand on her face. She hadn't meant it like that. She couldn't remember when someone touched her because they wanted to touch her. She had never been touched like that. But it wasn't that what terrified her. It was the fact that Elijah didn't only want to touch her, he looked like he needed to touch her. Desperately.

Hand frozen near her, he merely ghosted it where he had meant to touch her.

Rowan's eyes drew shut, her chest rising fast as if his hands truly were on her. She could feel them as if they were, and her teeth dug on her bottom lip, muting a gasp.

"Open your eyes for me," he said, and Rowan heeded to the order, not because she'd been used to obeying, but because she wanted to obey.

She had not realised up until then how much peace there was in the eyes of war. How calm the centre of chaos was. How soft anger could be. How gently did it look back at her. Ever since the day she was made part of this war, she'd never once wished or desired peace. She'd just realised why. Peace was just another war. And Rowan was losing it. She was losing her war.

"I'm not her," she shakily breathed.

"I know," he repeated again.

"Don't touch me like I'm her."

The violence in the violet of his eyes grew so weak, so pale. "I won't. I've never gotten this close to her before." His smile was shaky, unsure, almost stunned as he touched her. "I wouldn't know how anyone else feels. Only how you do."

Reaching a hand to his chest, she took a step forward, and then another. Until she was pressed to him, her cheek resting over his calm heart and her arms banded tightly around his hard body. Once his scent of sandalwood filled her lungs, she heaved a heavy sigh, suddenly all weightless and boneless before the last war she swore to ever fight.

"I've never given one of these before," she confessed, burying her face in his hold. "They're not so bad."

Gently, as if it could scare her away, Elijah put a hand around her, and then another, pulling her closer, tighter when she made no move to slip away from him.

It was the gentlest trap she'd ever fallen into.

A sight left her when he pressed his lips against the crown of her hair and then again on her brow.

"Why are you so quiet?" she asked, suddenly greedy for his voice to fill the space around her.

"I don't wish to scare you away."

"I am not scared." Her chest rose fast. "Maybe just a little."

Chuckling, he pressed his face to the crook of her neck, inhaling her and groaning. "Rowan, Rowan, Rowan."

His warm breath sent shivers down her spine, and the way he chanted her name made her breaths stutter. While his hard body pressed against hers did something else entirely. A myriad of things she had never felt before. Let alone all at once.

"Elijah?" she quietly asked, lifting her arms to wrap them around his neck, testing all the ways one could hold another.

"Yes, little thief," he answered, pulling her to him closer, her body melting against his hard, muscled one.

She could feel every ridge on his body, every little detail. Rowan had entirely forgotten her question. Rowan had sort of forgotten he was a man as well—well, for the most part, at least. "I...I can't remember what I wanted to ask."

A strange sound left her mouth when he kissed her neck, and yet again when he chuckled against her skin. Her thighs pressed together when she felt a strange wetness gathering between them.

"I think I'm going to pull away now," she said, starting to feel her body warm up unusually so.

He nodded. "I think it would be better."

"Really?"

"Unfortunately," he said, stretching his neck.

Awkwardly, she pulled back and fixed her shirt as she took a few steps away from him and spun to sit back on her bed.

"Who are you writing to?" he asked as she was about to fold the tenth letter back into its envelope.

"The queen."

"So many letters?"

"And her court."

His brows rose up. "What would you want all of them to know?"

"What they need to know from me. Reports."

"Reports, huh?" he asked, attempting to stretch in his tiny stool and almost falling from it.

She scooted back to one edge of the bed and pointed a finger to the other end. "Sit there."

Attempting to contain his amusement, he stood and sat where she had told him to sit. "Pity doesn't feel so bad."

Rowan smiled as she sealed her last envelope and placed the whole stack of them inside her bag before stuffing it under the bed. When she got up to get the map she needed to mark before handing it to Adam tomorrow, he groaned, forcing her to look back at him.

"Just sit with me. Deal with your little evil plans later."

"They aren't *little evil plans.*"

"I'm sorry," he crooned, urging her back to sit down, closer to him this time. "Not *little evil plans.*" He leaned in, brushing his lips on her cheek and then down her chin. "Big and bad evil plans."

She stopped him just as he was about to reach her lips, her fingers pressing to his mouth. Embarrassment burned over her cheeks. "I don't know how to do that." There was much Rowan was not taught, much she had not experienced, much she'd denied herself despite her age.

"I'm a very good teacher," he said, kissing each one of her fingers and pulling them away from his face to place them on his shoulders. "Have you ever danced, Rowan?"

"No."

"I will teach you that, too. This is also very much like a dance. One leads and the other follows," he said, leaning in until their lips were only a thin breath away. "It's just a dance, my little thief, you can breathe."

When she parted her lips to take a deep breath, he pressed his mouth to hers. Her eyes drew shut like his had, and her chest tightened, nerves pooling on her stomach. Unusual nerves. Nerves that turned something fierce when he sucked her bottom lip, when he breathed all of her breaths, when he shared his with hers. He groaned in her mouth when she began kissing him back, his skin shivering and pimpling with gooseflesh under her fingertips as she ran them up and down his nape.

Rowan followed his lead, and the kiss went from tentative to devouring soon after. She didn't not mind it at all.

Elijah's touch skittered down from her neck to her waist, and he pulled her surrendered body to his, setting her across his lap, her legs straddling his hips.

She gasped, feeling him beneath her, his hardness pressing between her legs. "I've not done that either."

"Would you want me to teach you that, too?" he asked, trailing his lips against her throat, and lowering his hands down her hips, pulling onto them slightly so she rocked against him.

"Yes," she breathed, her mouth parting with a silent gasp when the friction rendered her sight hazy.

He kissed her, hungrily this time, his tongue sliding against hers. Rowan almost couldn't keep up. And when he finally let her breathe, it was only to say something that rendered her breathless again, "Be the death of me, Rowan." His lips were on her face, on her neck, on her shoulder. "I want to die happy." He pushed her large sleeping shirt down her shoulders until it fell to pool around her waist, leaving her bare before him—the barest she'd been before a man, both heart and mind.

For a moment, she reached to put her arms over herself, but

held back because of how he was looking at her. It wasn't the look the other women who sometimes bathed with her gave her—the look full of disgust and pity.

No, this was entirely different. Rowan had to look down at herself to see if something had changed and she'd not noticed—to see if her scars had somehow magically disappeared. But they were still there. In fact, under the faint light inside the tent, they somehow looked even more gnarly. "Do you want me to blow off the lantern?" she asked, smoothing her clammy palms down her bedsheet, and hoping he'd say no.

"Why would I want that?"

She clung to her shirt that was still bunched around her waist, covering her stomach. "They only get worse from here down."

Something shifted in his eyes, making them turn a fierce shade of violet, almost a deep maroon. "Maybe you should," he said, and she felt herself fade a little. "I don't know if my eyes are deserving of you, Rowan. To behold something this beautiful."

Tears almost choked her words, "I am not—"

He kissed the rest of her words, trapping them in her lips so he could finish them himself, "Anyone else's but mine. No, you're not." He pushed her hair to the side, dragging kisses up her neck until she started writhing in his hold. "Finders keepers, Rowan of Ingburn." His lips found her ear, and he whispered, "So be mine. At least for tonight. Then I will beg yet again tomorrow. And the day after. And the day after that."

Her shaky hands began undoing his shirt, slipping and stumbling because of her clammy skin. When the last button came undone, she glanced down at him. "You really fooled me." She pushed his shirt off his thick, broad shoulders, watching the ripple of muscle shiver as she grazed her hands over his skin. "You really are no man."

His eyes drew shut, his breaths coming in shallow as her hands moved lower down his body. "I'll be whatever you want me to be. Man, God, both." He caught her hand and pushed it inside his trousers, her fingers sliding over his thick, hard length. "You make me feel like both. Man and God." He swallowed hard when she carefully wrapped her hand around him and slid it over his cock. "Rowan," he panted, his chest falling and rising fast. "Fuck, Rowan."

She didn't have the slightest clue what she was doing. She had not the slightest clue how she was making his body react to her so viciously. Or how he was making hers react either.

"Let me touch you," Elijah breathed, grazing the tip of his finger over her hard nipple, and making her gasp. Leaning in, he drew it in his mouth, sucking and licking until she was panting and squirming from the pounding ache between her thighs. "Let me make you feel good. Take your clothes off," he said, leaving wet kisses over her breasts.

Rowan slowly climbed off his lap and laid on her back, undoing her trousers and pulling them down her legs.

"Open them for me," he said, kissing her knees and trailing both his hands down her thighs, making her whole body tremble.

She was sure she'd gone red down her toes when she did so.

"Look at you, my beautiful Rowan," he cooed, kissing the inside of her scarred thighs, and making her skin hum.

"I want to see you, too," she managed to say, and he obeyed her request, sliding the rest of his clothes off. The odd God was made of thick, hard muscle everywhere, his skin scarred just like hers. She wondered if someone like him could even scar. There was very little time to marvel at his upper half. Because—

He chuckled when her eyes widened on his cock. "Do I need to go over the basics?" he asked, fisting himself and rubbing his hand down his length as he watched her head to toes.

"I know where it goes. It's just—"

"Just what?"

She'd been deceived by her sense of touch considerably. "It looks a bit...disproportionately big." The ones she'd unfortunately caught a glance off from careless soldiers were...smaller?

"It will fit."

Her knees buckled together. "What if it doesn't?"

Bending down, he left a kiss on each knee. "It will. You were made for me and I was made for you. It will." He smoothed his hands down her thighs, making her shiver. "Now open them so I can get a taste of you."

"A...a what?"

"What I've been wanting to do for a while," he said, kissing his way down her thighs, making her melt at his touch entirely, not even noticing how her legs fell apart for him. Not even noticing when his head lowered between them or when his tongue darted to lick her sex.

Her back bowed off the bed at the sensation and she sucked in a sharp breath. "Oh."

"Good *oh*, or bad *oh*?" he asked, pressing his fingers to the apex of her sex, and circling them along her core.

"Good," she moaned, her eyes squeezing shut. It had never felt as good as when she did it. Never. Not even nearly close enough.

Her hand shot to his brow when he sucked the tender spot where his fingers had been. His tongue lapped at her until her body was writhing restlessly on the thin mattress. "Elijah," she whimpered.

"Yes, my little thief," he cooed, pressing soft kisses to her sex before burying his tongue in her sensitive nerves again.

She felt a finger at her entrance and tensed as he pushed inside her, the sting making her clutch her bedding tightly in her fists until it almost tore.

"Relax for me, Rowan," he soothed, kissing her scarred stomach. "That is it. Good. Good girl."

Propping herself on her elbows, she looked down at this finger thrusting in and out of her. It was the single most titillating thing she had seen despite having the unfortunate luck of witnessing one too many soldiers carelessly fucking on every private space they could find.

He looked up at her, his chin and mouth glistening with her wetness. "My beautiful Rowan. All mine," he crooned. Lifting forward, he briefly pressed his lips to hers and then kissed his way down between her legs, only stopping to nuzzle her breasts.

Rowan could feel a tightening down her spine, curling like a tight spring waiting to be set loose. That feeling intensified, growing to be the most acute notion she had ever felt the more he lapped at her core, the more he pumped his thick, long finger inside of her.

She put a hand on his shoulder when it grew too unbearably intense. "Elijah—"

"Come, little thief, I want to taste you on my tongue."

Her teeth dug on her lower lip to drown her moans as she shattered to pieces, her entire body not feeling her own anymore.

"That's it," he hummed, his mouth still pressed against her sex until the last wave of lurid pleasure washed down her body.

Panting, she cracked her eyes open and looked down at him, shivering when he left one last kiss on her thigh and hauled himself over her.

Licking his lips, he smiled down at her as he rose to settle his big body over hers. His mouth fell on her cheeks, her eyes, her brow, her nose, and then her mouth. "This feels like the cruellest dream," he murmured over her skin as he marked every inch of her neck with his tongue.

"It can't be. I don't have dreams. Only nightmares. This doesn't feel like one. Not even remotely," she said, cupping his face and kissing him. When she pulled back, she noticed him watching her with an indecipherable look in his strange violet eyes. "What is it?"

"You kissed me."

She blinked up at him. "You started it."

He chuckled, brushing his nose against hers. "Exactly." Reaching a hand between them, he fisted his cock and rubbed the thick head along her entrance until she had the urge to beg and ask him to end her misery.

She felt the thick head push inside her and winced at the stretch. One slow inch at a time, he buried himself inside her.

She'd never felt so full, so impossibly full.

He groaned, his eyes turning that violent shade again. "Knew it would fit perfectly."

Her eyes screwed shut, and she shook her head, pushing at his shoulders.

"I am sorry," he breathed, nipping at her lips, leaving small pecks, gentle pecks, as he started slowly moving inside her. "I'm sorry."

The sensation didn't grow any less uncomfortable, but something else accompanied the stinging feel, something that had her eyes and mouth open both at once. She moaned as her body shifted in the mattress at his thrusts.

Bracing one forearm on the mattress, he lowered himself closer to her and took her mouth. "You feel so good, Rowan. So, so good," he murmured between kisses, reaching to palm her tender breast with his other hand. "Does it still hurt?"

She shook her head. The pain was dull and insignificant to what had taken over her entire body.

At her permission, his thrust found a new pace, making the sound of their bodies joining grow louder, venerous.

He groaned in her mouth. "Forgive me, little thief, but I've been celibate for too many lifetimes, and I don't think I can last much longer."

"Doesn't matter," she said, cupping his pained face. "I just wanted to be with you."

Pressing his brow to hers, he sighed, repeating her own words, "Don't do this to me."

"Do what?" she breathlessly asked, her fingers digging on his back with each thrust.

"Make me regret striking that deal for my life."

He took her body gently, slowing down, prolonging each and every shiver he created on her body with his touch, his lips, his cock filling her up. Tension pooled in her belly again, moving further down with each thrust, each kiss, at the feel of his palms cupping her breasts, his fingers playing with her taut nipples.

"Elijah, please," she moaned, her limbs growing restless, reaching, and tangling with his until they were as one.

To her luck, he obeyed her silent request, not holding back as he'd had. Their bodies rocked hard, the sounds that came out of them growing even louder, more desperate. She was grateful her tent was the furthest in the camp when she screamed as her climax rippled through her body again, even more viciously than before.

He slammed into her in one deep thrust and groaned in her mouth, nipping at her lips until their breaths synced to a normal pace. "Are we okay?" he asked, kissing both of her cheeks.

"Yes," she replied, wincing when he pulled out of her.

Pushing back to his haunches, he looked down at her still spread wide before him, his mouth pulling into a smirk. She might have rejoiced the same as him, but she was slightly stunned at the scene, at the blood between her thighs and on his cock, and his come seeping out of her.

When she tried to close her legs, he put a hand to her knee, stopping her. "Let me convince myself this happened."

She quickly pulled on a discarded sheet and threw it over her body, gathering herself tightly under it. "It happened," she said, pressing her face to her pillow as if it was enough to hide herself from him.

"Regretful?"

"No," came her muffled voice.

"Then what is it?"

She quickly glanced at him, and the blush creeping all over her face was enough of an answer for him because he chuckled.

"A little late to be embarrassed now," he said, laying behind her on her small mattress and pulling her body to his, wrapping her in a cocoon of his big limbs.

Yes, it was. Especially when she could still feel his come between her thighs and the soreness pounding there still. She'd never let anyone near her body the way Elijah had just been. She'd always been set in never allowing a man that sort of control over her. But she was enjoying his control over her.

He pressed his lips to her ear. "I plan on making love to you many more times before I'm ready for my death, so you're going to have to look at me at some point."

"Don't call it that," she murmured, trying not to shiver at his words.

"Call it what?"

"Love."

"But we didn't fuck, my little thief. You'll know the difference when I have you on all fours, your head buried in a pillow like now and your back arched as I bury my cock in your tight cunt from behind. You'll scream, and no one will hear you asking for me to fuck you harder."

Her thighs pressed together, and Elijah's hand rested against her stomach, his fingers tracing lines back and forth her skin. "You'd like that?"

Instead of answering, she buried her face in the pillow again, making him chuckle once more.

Ten poppies

ELIJAH WAS NOT BESIDE her when she woke up. And it felt strange after waking each day of the past week by his side, sharing his warmth, breathing in his scent, being held.

A pang of disappointment lodged in her chest the longer she waited for his return. She'd never been so jaded as when she got herself washed and dressed, her head turning towards the tent entrance from time to time, expecting him to return to her.

The second she poked her head out of her tent, she could sense the shift in the air, the coldness it carried. Yes, coldness. Less than half of the fires were lit that very chilly autumn morning.

She grabbed a passing soldier. "Where is everyone?"

"Down at the riverbank. They've finally managed to get the bridge over it."

No. No. No.

Horror washed over Rowan as she ran through the camp, directly towards the riverbank. From the far distance on top of the hill they had made their rest on, she could see the mass of soldiers dive into the dangerous water currents, carrying heavy logs. The sound of hammers echoed as they nailed down the feet of the bridge with ease, unlike what she'd told Henry and Adam.

While she'd been entirely too distracted with Elijah, they'd gone behind her back without her even noticing a thing. How far along her lie had they realised she'd been deceiving them? How much did they know? How much time had she left to act before it was too late for the Gobresh?

She couldn't spot Henry or Adam below with the soldiers setting up the bridge, so she spun and ran back towards their tents. Her feet came to a halt when Daniel came out of their tent, a strange look in his face. One that brightened when he noticed her in the distance. "Just who I was looking for," he shouted and waved, grinning at her.

His smile faded a little, and he sucked in a sharp breath. Rowan did so too when trails of blood gushed from the corners of his mouth as he looked down at his chest, at where a blade had pierced right through it from behind.

Rowan felt something fade in her chest. She became entirely unaware of her own body. Floating inside her own mind, drowning inside her own blood. Rowan lost something when Daniel raised his ebbing eyes up to hers again and smiled.

Adam pulled his sword back, wiping the bloodied blade on his sleeve as he shot Rowan a scathing look at the distance. "Traitorous vermin."

Daniel staggered on his feet, still refusing to surrender.

"Come on," Rowan bellowed, running towards him with all she had, forcing her own body to move—puppeteering her own limbs that no longer felt her own. "Come on!"

She reached him just as he fell to his knees, bracing his body in her arms before the cold earth could. Blood soaked her vision. Blood soaked her hands. The scent was assaulting her senses in a way it had never done before.

"I was...I was going to tell you," he choked, sputtering blood.

"I know. I know."

A sob broke his young face. "They wouldn't let me. They thought you would try to stop this. They...they think you've been delaying them on purpose. A-Adam had kept notes of you," he breathed, coughing blood. "To send to the queen and ask for your death."

"I know."

He laughed, tears pouring from his eyes, washing away the blood on his face. "Of course you do." A tremble overtook his limbs. "I confessed for you. I took all the blame."

Her stomach sank. "What?"

"They won't catch you. So do what you have to do quickly," he managed to say between short, sharp breaths.

Her face twisted in a cry. "Daniel." There were so many things she wanted to tell him. So many things she had to confess. So many simple words she'd wanted him to have. *I am proud of you. Well done. You've grown up so well.* But her throat had closed up.

"In another life," he said, the boy who'd come to her at merely eleven years of age, the boy she'd been raising for the past ten years. "In another life I want you to be my mother." He smiled at her, not like her captain, not like the soldier she'd trained and honed to kill, but like the boy he had never had the chance to be. "I'd ask of the Gods for you to be my sister, but we've bickered in this lifetime enough, so be my mother instead."

"I can't," she managed to say despite the tightening in her throat that was digging into her skin like barbed wire. "Forgive me, I don't think I can." Leaning in, she pressed her lips to his brow and whispered, "For I will lose the right to my soul after today."

He choked, his eyes drawing shut.

"Sleep now," she said, cradling his head on her lap, her own tears joining his.

Elijah had found her sitting before the grave she'd dug in the middle of the forest, between the flowers she'd buried Daniel in. "There you are," he murmured, pressing his lips to her temple, and sitting beside her.

Rowan was thinking.

When Rowan thought, bad things followed.

She allowed herself to lean against him, to let him hold her to his chest, to comfort her. "I'd planned for him to bury me instead."

He remained unusually silent as he held her to him tightly, the tightest he'd ever held her.

"Where were you?" she asked, pressing her ear to his heart, letting the slow rhythm calm her. Except, his heart wasn't calm like it usually had been. His pulse roared beneath her touch.

"I was called."

"By who?"

"*Death.*"

Something like fear chilled her blood. "Why? Why would he call for you?"

"My time might be running short."

She let out a stuttering laughter despite her tears. Standing on her knees, she cupped his face and kissed him. "I don't think so, Elijah. I think you're going to have a long, long life. And I think you're going to find her again in the next lifetime—alive, waiting for you. And you will tell her how you love her, and she will—" Her voice faded a little, drowned behind tears. "And she will tell you that she loves you back."

His own eyes filled with tears, too, as he lifted a hand to her face. "What a pretty tale."

"It isn't," she cried. "It isn't."

Rowan was thinking.

As she sat along her soldiers for the last dinner before the battle they would lead tomorrow towards Gobresh capitol, thinking was all Rowan could do.

She didn't touch her food just yet, her eyes taking in every soldier around her enjoying their last meal. Their boisterous voices and laughter filled her pockets with sin.

For every face she could see, she wondered what future they would have, she could see their youths slipping to adulthood. She could imagine them with their own families, falling in love, ageing slowly with those they loved. For the hour she'd stood there, she'd given everyone a life they would never have so she could feel guilt kill her slowly. For she deserved the cruellest way to die.

The twenty letters she had written to her queen and her court had been sent early that morning, and by the next morning, Mugril capital would have all learnt of the new world that would rise from the ashes of the old—from the ashes of the fire Rowan would soon burn.

Elijah came to take a seat beside her, and that moment had been the only time she'd felt a pang of regret at what she was about to do. Her eyes drew shut when he took her hand in his, lacing their fingers together. Every little touch marking her sinful soul.

"Not that," she said, putting a hand over his water cup and switching it with another. Her voice shook as she said, "Drink from this."

His eyes bore into hers. Somewhere between the look they exchanged he'd found her soul and bid it goodbye—there was goodbye in his voice too when he said, "As you wish, my Rowan."

A sob raked through her chest as she also raised her cup to her lips. She pressed a trembling hand to her mouth, forcing herself to swallow her fate.

"You did it," he said, watching her like he was doing it for the last time, with a look so sombre, so tender, so fragile that it almost hurt her to die. Such a look that she might have died once already.

It almost made her wish she'd made an antidote for the poison she'd just drank. Almost. Only almost. Because she remembered that he'd now get to live again, that his bargain with the Gods of Life and Death had been made void since she'd die before she'd get to kill him.

"I can finally tell you this," he said, wiping away her tears.

"Tell me what?" she asked, suddenly panicked that there was no time for her to hear what he had to say, afraid the poison would take in too quickly.

"That I've found you in every lifetime. In every lifetime I've watched you die. In some you've died in my arms, too. Those are the ones I remember the most. You never remembered me. You don't remember me still. You won't remember me. I hope you won't."

Rowan couldn't move.

No.

It didn't make sense.

"No," she whispered. "No, I am not her."

Blood suddenly streamed down the corner of his mouth. "My heart was yours from the start and until the very end."

Rowan jumped back, her eyes wide, her limbs shaking. Fear, not poison, they were shaking from fear as she picked up the cup he'd drank from, the only cup she had not laced with the haleberry poison. The bottom of it had turned a burnt red, the metal oxidising from the poison. "No, no, no," she frantically chanted as she reached for hers, noticing the clear bottom that had not stained—the cup she had meant for him. "No. Please, no. Don't do this to me!"

Elijah coughed, blood sputtering from his mouth.

She grabbed his body before it crashed to the ground. "I'm not her," she muttered, swaying the two back and forth. "I'm not her!"

"No, you're not. Happens to the best of us. We change." He

lifted a weak hand to her face. "You changed. You changed so much, my little thief. If you didn't look like my every dream, my biggest wish, my utmost desire, I wouldn't have recognised you in this lifetime. I knew something was different. I knew this would be my last life the moment I recognised you. You cheated the Gods and the Fates this time." His thumb brushed her eye. "You buried your soul so deep in there that they all thought you had died already."

She cried, her chest burning with painful sobs. "It can't be. Why can't I remember? I want to remember. Please!" she begged. "Please, I want to remember!"

"I begged that you wouldn't. I begged them so you wouldn't carry this pain that I carried. Time took your memories. But I have them all."

"You're a God," she cried. "You're a God, you can't die! Please, Elijah."

"You were like the sky to me, my Rowan." He touched a blood-stained palm to her cheek so tenderly. "Ever so blue, ever so exquisite, ever so far away from me."

Life disappeared from his violet eyes as he drew them shut, his hand slipping away from her face, and his body surrendering.

Rowan held her shivering breath.

And then she screamed, begging someone and anyone for help. But no one heard her as she laid in a graveyard of her own people. The night was silent. The most silent it had ever been. The only beating heart remaining for far and long miles was the one in her chest. Every other one had already gone to sleep forever, too weak to have survived the poison that Rowan had laced their food and their water with.

It had to stop.

One way or another.

She couldn't remember how many times she had calculated the least cruellest way possible to end it. But this had been the only solution that had come up with every equation she'd solved. The price for the peace she had brought would be severe—she'd always known it. But she'd not accounted for this. The silent soul she held in her arms.

"It should have been your heart beating," she cried, laying down with him. Taking his cold hand, she put it to her chest. "This is yours, so maybe it still is."

The ground beneath them cracked loudly, and she hugged Elijah's body to hers, closing her eyes and waiting for the moment she would join him. The earth and sky alike rumbled, trees and rocks shook and violently quivered as a quake took over the land. One she'd never witnessed before.

It might have lasted hours or days, Rowan couldn't remember.

But the moment the earth had fallen silent, she'd buried the owner of her heart. It had taken a long while for her to leave his side. And as the poppies had grown over his grave, she'd given in on her grief and cried for days to no end until her soul had consumed itself entirely, and she felt numb.

On the thirtieth day after, his sword had shown itself at her feet when she had woken.

Dawnbringer had turned a pale shade of silver, almost white. The red rubies at the hilt gleaming in contrast.

With it on her back, she'd ridden towards Gobresh, only to find the river that used to separate their land was now a sea instead. She couldn't see where the space of water ended. And no matter how far along the old riverbank she had ridden, how many days she'd searched back and forth, she couldn't find any land connecting to Gobresh.

Tisiania had parted in two. That had been the only explanation she could come up with.

She'd left his grave again. She swore it would be the last time. When she would return, she would join him.

Her hood drawn over her face and *Dawnbringer* on her back, she'd weaved through the streets of Mugril. Her homeland that she'd not seen in years. A gloom had fallen over her people as they went about their business.

For a while, Rowan had stood in front of the royal palace. Reading the order that had been posted on its gates. A new queen had taken over after the previous had died, poisoned in her own bed, her letter between her fingers and the truth becoming her gravestone. A new court had been formed after they, too, had died the moment they'd touched her letter laced with the haleberry powder. The Mugril had mourned their lost soldiers and they'd taken an oath to repent for the sins committed in their names and had sworn to never cross the waters separating the two kingdoms.

Peace had won.

At a cost.

A terrible, terrible cost.

With tears in her eyes, Rowan had read the order until her feet had bled holding her upright. And then she'd returned back to him.

Word had it that she'd laid between the poppies, and the flowers had taken pity on her and sung her a lullaby of death until the God had come to take her to the afterlife, too. They say the dark God had been cruel to her. For the millions of innocent lives she'd sent to his world, he'd gifted Rowan her lover's immortality, a life of eternal repentance. He'd denied her greatest wish. Liberation.

Instead, when she'd risen again, she'd found herself in another lifetime.

And many more endless ones.

Alone.

And without war.

Without him.

She was alone with the memories of every lifetime she'd lived before since the start of it all. And like he'd said, they'd tormented her.

Epilogue

SHE HAD WAITED FOR him at the edge of every lifetime. All thousands of them. Sometimes he'd come to her on a white horse, sometimes he'd come to her through a body of mist. Smiling like only he could.

But only in her dreams.

There was no *turmoil* and *tranquil*.

There was no war or peace.

There had been just him and her. Two people who'd met at the dawn of time. Two people who'd made an unbreakable bargain. There wasn't one without the other. One couldn't exist without the other. At least she hoped that was the case.

Now, as she stood before the blinding sun still rising east despite all her prayers, full of memories she'd carried through days and nights, she watched a young girl and boy who gazed at the orange skies making bargains and promises of their own.

She would wait for him at every sunrise. Thousands more. And he'd come to her in more than dreams. He'd come to her.

He would find her as he had always found her.

Hope was all that she had left.

That and the exact colour of his eyes. She saw it everywhere. The violet twilights, the spring crocuses and hyacinths, the trails of amethysts in wind torn rocks, the ocean at sunset, the skies after a storm.

Even her hope was violet. The most violent kind.

She was glad this story had no ending at all, because one way or the other, they were bound to have a chance to actually end it.

"You're her," a cold, dark voice called from behind her, and she froze, waiting for her mind to stop dreaming.

It had been far too long of a time to remember his voice so well. And she'd fallen prey to the Gods of Deceit too many times to allow herself to hope.

When she turned, he stood there, like every other dream. Violent violet eyes and all, and staring at her with so much hate—staring at the sword she carried on her back.

When she'd been passed Dawnbringer by the Gods, Rowan had learnt that peace was just another war. That she was a cruel God like the rest. One who deserved the hate in the eyes of the man who still held her heart.

"I am," the Queen of Gods said, feeling tears streaming down her face. "I am," she repeated, smiling at him, knowing he would never smile back at her.

Maybe their story never had an end because the red string of fate tied to them always tangled when they met in the middle.

Maybe it was because of the cruel bargain they'd made once too many dawns ago.

Maybe because mankind would always fight, whether there was war or peace, whether there was him or her.

About the Author

Wendy Heiss is an indie author debuting with a new adult fantasy trilogy. Winter Gods & Serpents is the first book in The Auran Chronicles, releasing autumn 2021. She has graduated with honours in Forensics Science in the United Kingdom, but literature has been one of her passions since she could manage to read and write. Despite being severely tempted to ride the Agatha Christie route to crime novels, she chose to follow the Tolkien path to fantasy. She forwent fingerprint powder for ball pen ink, inevitably forgoing her parents' hope for a good life and becoming what they always feared...a figuratively starving artist.

Any whom and how, she likes cats, coffee, particularly that cr*p from instant sachets. Claims to despise mafia romance from the pits of her gall bladder but will probably end up writing one herself to try and outwrite the greatest line in history: Are you alright baby girl.

Also, fried sweet potatoes, she can definitely eat some of those without claiming to be allergic to yet another vegetable. On that last note before straying too far from a simple bio, please read her book and more to come.

Acknowledgements

First and foremost, thank you to my readers, there are so many of you now that I can't even believe myself when I see your comments all over my social media. We are on book 5, can you even believe this????? You all have made this possible.

Jada, thank you for letting me rant to you always.

Neta, bestie!! Thank you a billion times for just being there since we were both miserable and moaning about unbearable co-workers. I'm so proud of you for finishing school and becoming a midwife.

My sister, thank you for being the little yet helpful menace that you are. Hope you will outlive me because I really couldn't even bear to think you might not.

Afterword

Hello everyone, there was a little something I wanted to share with you.

These books are short. I know. I also have taken in all the feedback my readers have sent me and I do understand you wish they were longer and more detailed, but I do want to say that my intention with this series was to write them as fairy tales are written. The initial inspiration came from the Grimm Fairy tales (which I was reading as part of research for my other series, Daughters of Chaos). My intention was to replicate something similar, but with romance and characters as a main focus, so if you have noticed, I've left most conflict entirely out of the plot as they could have essentially been anything and would have still not changed a thing to the story. Could these books be longer? Definitely. I can easily make these novellas three, four, five hundred pages and probably even more if my editor would let me. However, I feel that the length is appropriate for what I am trying to convey. There is no such thing as falling in love too quick or not quick enough. There is no such thing as a love story being too short or too long. That is the magic of storytelling, and the magic of love, too.

If I have failed to make you believe these love stories, that is not the fault of the page count, that is mine. The good thing about being an author is that you learn and you grow and you perfect your craft with each and every story you tell, so I do hope that one day I can make you believe a one page long love story.

And remember, not every story has to end happily for it to be a love story. The greatest love stories have always ended in tragedy.

Also By

The Auran Chronicles
Winter Gods & Serpents
Spring Guardians & Songbirds
Season Warriors & Wolves
Autumn Queens & Shadows
Summer Heirs & Fire (coming soon)
Daughters of Chaos
City of Alabaster (coming soon)
Blue Fairytales
At the end there was you
The last war we ever fought
Where the light no longer follows

Next standalone novella in the series...

Time no longer exists. At least not to Silene.

Serving under the God of Death as a Reaper, she finds herself stepping between life and death every day, collecting souls and guiding them towards the afterlife. When the brother of Death begins interfering in her duties, she begins to question her existence and purpose.

And the closer she comes to finding her answers, the further her current reality sinks deeper.

www.ingramcontent.com/pod-product-compliance
Lightning Source LLC
Chambersburg PA
CBHW060353180626
46817CB00008B/2999